JIM MORGAN AND THE MANIFESTATION OF PLANETS

JIM MORGAN AND THE MANIFESTATION OF PLANETS

BHARAT MADAN

BOOKS WAGON

BOOKSWAGON

Jim Morgan and the Manifestation of Planets

Edition 2018

Published by
Bookswagon
www.bookswagon.com
An Imprint of
SR Ecommerce Factory Pvt. Ltd.
2/14, Ground Floor Ansari Road, Daryaganj,
New Delhi–110002, India.

customerservice@bookswagon.com
Ph.: 01141521153, 40159253

Ordering Information : Visit our website **www.bookswagon.com**

Printed at
Radha Press, Site 4, Sahibabad (U.P)

For you Mom and Dad

Thank you for believing in me and my work.

Thank you Krati, Mudrika and Vanshika. Without you guys, this book wasn't possible.

What would I do without you guys- Nikhil, Shikhar and Naman (The Singles).

Chapter 1

It was nearing two hours past the last minute of Jim Morgan's interaction with his fans in a popularly arranged New York Auditorium. Jim, sitting at the center chair where all eyes were on him, was waiting for a signal from Noah, wondering when she would tell the media that the time for the interaction is over and then he could go back home where he would have dinner with his wife and daughter.

The readers couldn't get enough of him; they wanted more. For a year now, books and readers didn't get much of his time as he didn't leave a space in his life for anything other than family. So it was obvious, he had to spend extra hours to compensate for his public absence.

Every once in a while he would look at her sitting at the front seat but she didn't give him what he wanted. At last he realised that she wasn't going to say so for at least one more hour. Amidst the next few questions, he decided that he would call it a day. He looked at the host sitting next to him first and then to the audience. Then he spoke, 'I had a great time interacting with you and woah', he looked at his watch deliberately, 'I didn't realise when the time flew. I so wish to stay and just keep talking but you know before being Jim Morgan, I am a husband and the call of a husband goads me to say that I will take just one more question for tonight. After that I will be heading home, where an interrogation by yours very Mrs Morgan is nicely cooked and will be served for my being behind the dinner schedule. So I hope you wish me luck with that'. What followed was a short laugh and excitement in the crowd as all of them raised their hands for their chance.

'Definitely Jim, we wanted to spend more time and you just reminded me that somebody's waiting for me too. I don't want to be late else two public figures will face that interrogation tonight and everyone knows who wins. *The wife!*' He saidthrough lip-syncing and exaggerated drama. Everyone got his point. 'Okay I was going to say can we have a show of hands for the last question but since everyone's got their hands up, I will let Jim do the handpicking'.

Jim moved his eyeballs after the host on everyone to select the last one and he saw so much of desire on everyone's face, which made it difficult for him to pick. He took a few seconds and decided he would let the host choose for him. But just as he was about to turn to him, someone from the audience stood up. Everyone's eyes turned to this person and as Jim saw him, his pulse quickened. The host spoke, 'I guess that saves us the tag of being biased. So we have the last person to ask Jim something this evening. Yes sir so what would you like to ask?'

The person didn't speak and so did Jim. The man's face was cheerful and there was sparkling smile that no one had ever seen. Jim's was that of marked surprise. He was at a loss to explain to himself why he didn't see that face in the crowd of a hundred in the past four hours. A rush in the many thoughts that emanated in his mind within countable seconds stole the sense of comfort from him.

Have I not paid for my sin? Why are you here? Should I be glad or terrified? That smile, that same smile. Maybe I am in trouble. Or maybe he just came to say hello. It has been a year now. What now?

'Your seventh book, *Sins of Time* was really mysterious and intriguing. It ended at the point where the protagonist answered the entire questions in the chamber of planets. What if beyond that point, the planets are set loose and they took human form?' asked the person whom everyone in the crowd thought to be a man. But it was Jim who recognised that face. He was the originator of all, the source of all sources. God's words had struck a fear in him and suddenly, Jim stiffened, staring out at him with startled eyes. He had brought the news to him at a place and time least expected. The crowd could not make out the cause of the silence that followed between them.

The same words began swirling through his mind without giving the slightest trace of what was about to happen next in his peaceful life. The shuddering thought of God's presence again meant another quest for him; it was the same he felt a year ago when he chose to redeem his sins. Only this time, it wasn't limited only to his Karma. Manifestation of planets in human form could only mean that it had grown darker and powerful; the extent of it not yet imaginable. The moment pierced his heart with uncertainty.

Jim could not answer. For him, the question meant a quest which God had set for him. *What if the planets are set loose and they take human form?*

'Now that would make for a great eighth book', finished God and the lights went out. When they came back, he wasn't there. More than the crowd, Jim Morgan sat shocked.

Chapter 2

It was exactly five in the morning. Jim was released from the same dream that had been haunting him for some time now. He came out in the open yet his thoughts were dark. The visions he saw in the dream had deepened in his mind and they were flashing again and again before him. The wind was dead and so was any noise that could make its way to his ears. No insect of the night or animal were to give him company. Standing and strolling alone in the garden under the shade of the night, he met the same feeling which he met last year. The grim feeling had gripped him. It was whispering to him about a quest he must embark on. But he wasn't prepared and he didn't know where to begin. The attachment of a family life had held him tight; his heavy heart was not allowing him to accept his destiny.

Why must I go? Have I not paid for my sin?

The darkness before the light of the morning was dismal. Something was not usual, something was not right. The wind blew unnaturally; it went by. And then he heard a voice from behind. 'Yes you have!' He turned in an instant. 'And you must not decline from accepting the fact that you were present in the chamber of planets and that it was you who activated them'.

'How could I know that the planets will be set loose once they are brought to life using the seven keys? And even if I knew that, I still didn't have a choice. I had to save myself or I would have gone to hell. Choice was just an illusion, wasn't it'?

'You still can't make up your mind whether this is a result of fate or your karma. You had a choice and you took your chance. You of all should know that every action has a consequence'.

'You weren't like this the last time. You guided me. I knew what I was supposed to do'.

'And what do you think I am doing now? I also had a choice, and look, here I am in front of you, warning you of a certain catastrophe that will shake this Earth'. For the first time in this quest, Jim learnt that this one wasn't about him. Even though he understood that God didn't come to him because his debt to his sin was left unpaid, he could hardly take a breath after hearing this. 'If you choose not to do anything, then you will enjoy your life as it is but only for a very limited time. After that you will feel the greatest peril which humanity will face'. Part of him wanted to learn more and walk on the path God was about to show him; part of him wanted God to stop as listening to this was becoming unbearable to the peaceful man. God lessened the space between them and now they stood face to face. 'It will be the end of the world as you know it'. He froze as he heard those words and in God's eyes he could see the reflection of his own terrified look.

The same unnatural breeze came and swiftly took God away with it. Jim turned his gaze away from the place where God stood a few seconds ago and began to walk to his study. It was only there that he thought his mind would be able to think straight. On the chair before the window where he always wrote, he went on to struggle with a decision he wasn't willing to take. The last words of God weighed upon his head. Soon it was the sunrise hour. The darkness finally sank into the light of the sun which stretched to all directions. And only as the first light entered the room did Jim's reluctance left him. He made up his mind to set a brief farewell to his peaceful life that moment. Casting aside his sentiments for the sake of his family was what he chose to do. The door was ajar and he didn't notice Kathryn coming in.

'You look tired and worried'.

'Yes. Tired out with the nightmares and the contemplation'.

'What's wrong dear?'

'These nightmares, they mean something'.

'And what are you contemplating about?' Jim didn't speak. His choice had him unsettled. 'There's something you're not telling me'.

It was difficult to put all the thoughts together and narrate to her. Jim felt uneasy as he said, 'He came back'.

'He came back?' She was puzzled. The worry on his face could only mean one thing. After a very brief moment she spoke, 'You talked to God'. Jim's head shot up at Kathryn. He was surprised to find that she would know that quickly.

'He was different this time. He made me feel that he was disappointed in me'.

Kathryn sat by his side, on the large arm rest. 'Why do you think he made you feel that? He came to meet you. If he wanted he would have made you travel to the far end of the world to meet him'.

'End of the world', repeated Jim. He left a deep sigh and mustered courage to share with her. 'What would I do withoutyou? I was alone and look what I began thinking. You're right, he sees hope in me and I was thinking about disappointment'.

'It's okay Jim. We make mistakes. This makes us human. What did he tell you?'

'I saw him in an event a month ago. Disguised as a regular audience member, he asked me a question—What if the planets are set loose and they take human form?'

It was difficult for her to respond in a way that would soothe him. She still tried, 'They're Demi- Gods, the planets; they are up there to regulate the Earth and people in their everyday lives. Wouldn't they continue doing that?'

'We can't say anything yet. Not till we encounter them or understand at least something. I think my nightmares have got something to do with this'.

'What do you see in them?'

'I see a wanderer, cloaked in white robe, facing the great full moon all alone. I feel the pain of this person. I see a weak man, tied in chains; I can see electric shocks burning him and I can hear his screams. I see a soldier, preparing for an assault and his own men conspiring to kill him. I also see a man sitting on a green chair; he is the only one who seems fine to me but then a headless shadow looms over him. There's a saint trapped somewhere; the only company to him is a tree. A lady who is getting dissolved in a glass made of diamond and people surrounding her are relishing her misery. Lastly, there's a shadow. As soon as I try to reach him, a solar flare blinds me and the shadow vanishes. Next thing I remember is waking up from that nightmare. What terrifies me is that each time they came, they were exactly the same'.

'Are these visions related to what God told you?'

Jim let his breath out once again before he spoke. 'I must be fooling myself. Kathryn, planets took human form; I think they are in some danger and they need me. I feel these visions are sent to me by some force, maybe God or someone else which wants me to do something'.

Kathryn felt that he was hiding something from her. She took a moment before she asked further, 'What else did you see?'

She was right. Jim didn't want to answer. It was the worst sight of all. Mere thinking about it gave him the feeling of the loss of everything. At last he spoke with an effort. 'I saw you and Leia drown in a lake of darkness. Every time, I try reaching out for you, but I can't. Something stops me and I lose you two'.

At this point, Kathryn held his hand tightly. 'You're not going to lose us. Nothing's going to happen to us. I know you and I know that you've already made up your mind to go on this quest, not because that is what you must do but you choose to do, for us'.

'Yes, I have. God also told me that humanity will face its greatest peril and life as we know it will end if I don't do something about it. I don't understand. What can I do alone? What must I do?'

Suddenly as he told her everything, an answer struck her. 'If we don't understand something we go to someone who can help us understand'.

'Who do I go to? Only you and Marshal believe that I can see and talk to God'.

'Then you must go to him. I know that I might not be helpful to you. But Marshal, he's a detective now. Maybe he will have some answers for you'.

'There's one more thing I need to know. God said that I have limited time. How much, he didn't say. He left before I could ask him anything'.

'Then you take the first flight to meet him. I will inform him that you're coming'. She got up to reach for her phone in the bedroom. Jim caught her hand right as she got up.

'I wish I could live life like the way it was. I do not want to leave you and Leia'.

She drew near him and wrapped him in her arms. 'Your quest awaits you Jim. I want you to set things right. I don't know how you're going to do it but I can tell you this. I am with you and so is Leia. Come back for us. We need you'.

As he looked at Kathryn, it occurred to him that he might not be seeing her and Leia again soon. The flight was booked. Till the time for his departure, he had his eyes watching over Leia and Kathryn like it was the last time he was going to see them. That had Kathryn worried but Jim finally took the first step of his journey. *I don't know when I will come back or what will happen but I want to take a good look at you two before I go.* Sebastian started the car and he sat back, watching the two disappear from his vision as the car turned left from the gate of his mansion.

Chapter 3

The first hour was very comfortable on the plane. Jim had occupied himself with the thought of his next novel. He had a pen and a diary but there was no drop of ink yet that fell on the first page. An air hostess brought a boy next to him. Apparently this boy was disturbing a female co-passenger and was requested to be shifted somewhere else. Luckily for the boy, he got promoted to the business class where only the window seat next to Jim's wasn't occupied.

'Sir this is a good seat that we can offer you. But I must request you to follow flight etiquettes'.

'Okay lady, I will make myself comfortable here. You can leave'. He looked at Jim who was busy pondering. 'Yo man! That's my seat', he said. Jim didn't look up. His mind was fixed on a thought but his ears told him that for the rest of the journey, a young, carefree and seemingly ill-mannered boy will give him company.

'This is the business class. There's enough space for you to go there without having me to get up', responded Jim. The boy was chewing a gum and watching him do it with a consistently opening mouth wasn't a pleasant sight for anyone. The hostess left them.

'Oh yeah, sure thing man'. He helped himself with the bag as he placed it on the top and sat there. 'Yo what's up, man? My name's Joshua', he stretched his hand. Jim, out of courtesy finally looked at him and shook hands with him. 'What're you writing over there?' he saw an empty page. 'Looks like the exam paper. Mine's always the same—empty'. Jim flitted a fake smile and went back to his thoughts. Joshua pressed the switch for the hostess. 'Let's see what we get here'. The same hostess came and this time Joshua looked at her badge for her name. 'Sara is it! What can you offer for drinks?'

'Sir, complementary drinks are offered to the business class passengers. You have been shifted here and since you're underage, I will have to decline'. She didn't want to attend him much and so she walked away.

'You see mister. She digs me', he punched Jim a little but he declined paying attention. It was precisely this sort of behaviour which made him worry about the future of next generation kids. But of course, Jim met a great deal of bright students and also offered them literature-learning opportunities. Joshua was the exact opposite—an ignorant school kid who steals from parents for his own amusement. At least for the next twenty minutes the latest movie on the screen in front of them caught Joshua's interest. Not able to write anything, Jim closed his diary and put it to the side. The movie was related to mutants and that caught Jim's interest too. They became occupied watching it.

But a few minutes later, Joshua's screen turned black. He stared pressing buttons. 'What's this? The screen isn't working'.

'Mine neither', said Jim. He reached for the switch on top of him and pressed it gently. It turned green. The hostess at her end got a short tone which meant a passenger required assistance. She got up and what followed surprised her. There were many short tones one after the other. Everyone had green lights on top of them. It seemed that there was a technical issue with the screens. It was the first time she witnessed such a peculiar instance. She took the announcing receiver in her hand to call her assisting hostess at the other end but before she could, one hostess from the other end came towards her. 'Sara, none of the screens are working. I have told a few passengers that we are seeing to it. Do you have any idea what is to be done?'

Sara, even though she was a senior, didn't remotely know. Then all the green lights turned off. Jessica turned back at Sara, 'Did you?'

'No I didn't. Let me ask the pilot about this'. She went inside the cockpit and came back half a minute later. 'They are saying it is something technical that can't be helped till we land'.

'It is going to be a very tough for us if we have to tell the passengers to bear till we land'. As they were discussing, a man approached the toilet. Luckily for them, he wasn't concerned about the problem. He just wanted to use the lavatory. There was already one occupied on his left, the other was vacant. As he stretched his hand to push the door, there was a sudden jerk that the plane felt; strong enough to send the hostesses and the man losing their balance.

'What was that?' asked Joshua. Everyone was alarmed. Jim looked at the hostesses and just as he did there was another powerful jerk that the plane felt.

'Is there something wrong miss?' Joshua was too loud. Sara told Jessica to go back and see that everyone's on their seat. The man occupying the lavatory barely got out of it and the other strived to balance himself up while the plane lost some altitude. 'Please go back to your seats sir', she said weakly with what she hoped was a relaxed and controlled facial expression. The two hurried back to their seats, stumbling as they went.

With a slight shiver, Joshua quickly fastened his seat belt. He was a little afraid of flight traveling and now his fear was worsening. Jim looked out the window, he could see the unexpected descent of the airplane as it now reached the clouds from far above. Then came the most powerful jerk, strong enough to spread chaos inside. It was then he heard a shriek from few seats behind him. Few bags fell on some passengers from the overhead cabin. The lights went out and the emergency blue light strip under the aisle seats came into life. Jim watched them from his feet to the spot where Sara was standing. But she wasn't on her feet. She quickly tried to get back to her position and talk to the pilots about this.

There had been no communication from the cockpit to the passengers in a grave situation like this. Sara quickly went inside and came back in another second. 'Oh God! I don't want to die like this', said Joshua loud enough for people to hear him. Jessica came somewhat rushing towards Sara. Jim had been afraid of that. Her sudden movement would only add to the panic of passengers. Joshua's heart sank. He started saying prayers.

'Sara the others are taking care of the passengers but everyone's frightened'.

'Don't worry, everything will be fine', she said, trying to sound braver than she felt. But her expressions betrayed a flicker of terror she had in her. What else would she do in a situation like this other than to try and calm the already panicked hostess! For a brief moment, she gave her the impossible hope that they will be safe.

Jessica was new to the aviation industry; not experienced to handle this kind of situation well. She shouted, 'Tell me what they're saying'.

Sara couldn't lie anymore. Marked fear had formed on her now. 'Nothing's working inside. The systems are dead. We might crash', she was too direct. Jim watched Jessica run into the economy and he knew there was something extremely wrong about it.

Sara also began to rush from the first class to the business. 'Everyone, please fasten your seat belts and lower your heads into your laps. The plane may lose altitude heavily. We must', she was about to say *brace for impact* but before she could there was a sudden drop in the height of the plane. It was as if there was a free fall.

Then began a great commotion. People started screaming. 'I don't want to die like this', Jim turned to see Joshua convinced that they were going to crash. The oxygen pipes fell down, and they dangled as the altitude dropped suddenly. 'We're going to die', shouted someone. That was the big thought that would come to the common mind. But Jim's was different. His body had instinctively followed the safety protocol. He quickly turned his head down on his lap; his mind however was wandering, trying to reach the root of the cause. *We can clutch our hands on hope for some mental support. But if a planet is behind this, there isn't a thing we humans could do to stop it.*

And as that thought came to him, almost immediately the lights came back. The pilots inside the cockpit saw life coming back into the systems and instantly they took control.

'Take it up', he said to his co-pilot. His voice was crisp and decisive. The altitude of the plane was carefully controlled and all communications with the destined air traffic controller was established again. 'Check the controls'.

The co-pilot took a careful look at them all. 'Jesus! They're all back to normal sir. It is as if nothing happened'.

'It is best that we land at the earliest. See if we have clearance for landing. I will maintain the normal course of our flight'.

Jim looked around the plane and saw mournful faces. Even though the pilot had given certainty of safety through an announcement, it would take more than a while after they touch land for the shock to wear off.

Joshua was still counting his prayers and his face was all covered with sweat. He would definitely remember this accidental adventure till his dying day like many others who were terribly shaken. Jim however, was wondering why it happened at the very beginning of his quest. *Was this the result of a huge scheme of destruction or was I being targeted?* But he was certain of one thing, right after he accepted that he couldn't do a thing against the threatening planet, the danger had left them. Maybe someone wanted that particular thought to come to his sense. Questions, more questions accompanied his mind till the plane landed. As it did, Jim saw several firefighting trucks, police wagons and other rescue operation teams assemble near other flights. It wasn't only their plane that had a temporary failure in their system. The attack was widespread.

*****

'What's been happening here?'

'Sir, one comes, one leaves and all of them have the same question. First the schedule board went haywire in the early afternoon. The systems failed to respond. It had been like this in all air and rail systems. We know only God saved us today. Whatever it was, some sort of electro-magnetic pulse or system crashing virus, it only happened for a few minutes and then everything recovered itself. I don't know who or what did it. People are saying it is a cyber-attack by terrorists'.

The world around him went mad; people were rushing to the nearest airline personnel, security officers with questions. Everyone behind the desk was clueless, the more they called senior officials for answers, the more confusion they got in response. Nobody could comprehend the sudden upheaval in the system.

Jim looked at the schedule board. It flashed correct display of departures and arrivals and people got their accurate information of their desktops. But they were left worried. Not sure whether it would happen again or not. Major television sets displayed reporters covering the news. Someone from New York, someone was LA, somewhere from some other place.

'I don't like this', he said to himself. 'Maybe it has already started—the end'. As he began walking out of the airport he overheard some news anchor asking a certain passenger about the recent hick-up of the internet, in one of the hanging television. He stopped along with many others.

'Is the internet in danger?' asked the anchor from the invited expert.

'No such possibility exists given the tech giants controlling most of the traffic. These hick-ups are a result of the increasing data uploading and grid buffering…' Jim couldn't understand the complexity of his narration but he knew that the expert was sent by the government to cover a lot. 'We have everything under control now', was what he said at last.

They know nothing about the problem and how the manifestation of planets had resulted in it.

Jim had a clue about how the situation of that place was. But he didn't know exactly how tormenting it would turn out during summers. It was a Sunday afternoon. Feeling that Marshal might know something about what happened, he made it to the outside of the airport. Within minutes, he was covered in sweat owing to the infamous hot temperature and he wished to enter the first one to beat the heat. 'Curse this heat', he muttered. 'First the plane and now this. Just keeps on getting worse'.

Standing right before an arriving car, a drop of sweat reached the end of his jaw; the fiery winds of the summer afternoon seared his face and part of hands that were left bare. At the sight of the first car coming towards him, he took a sigh of relief. Just before he pulled the front door, he took a look around. A nasty sight sent him in a shock. His jaw dropped a little. He saw people around him sweltering with temperature breaking all-time high records.

Old rock ranch was hot, but never this much. He couldn't bear the sight of such a crowd but his reflexes involuntarily tossed his body inside the cab. He settled to sit upright facing the AC vent just inches before it. He closed the door and got a feeling that he was advancing into a journey of ordeal.

'I'm here to meet someone. Here's the location'. He handed over the phone with the location to the driver. The car started to run; he turned around and started observing the view through the eyes of a disturbed commuter. At 1830 hours, he saw the brightest of the blue sky. Through the window, he gained vision of majestic lush green trees of the airport; they were reduced to skeletons; even the strongest trees withered. Varieties of plants half scorched, half kept alive by the contracting shadows of struggling tall trees; a few lingered waiting for their time to come. Blistering sun had been splitting the trees almost every day.

Jim struggled as he tried to link the cause of the unprecedented rise in temperature to the manifestation of the planets. He looked around as he adjusted himself to sit. He caught a glimpse of a newspaper kept on the pocket of a seat. It was filled with 'scores of people suffer in heat' stories. Pictures of animated sun beating, sucking planet Earth were prominently inserted in the paper. He held it and turned a few pages. *Exposure to hot airstreams disposes people to several infections central to which is heat stroke.*

'Has it been like this forever?' he asked the driver.

'Looks like you haven't been reading the newspaper sir. It has been like this for a year now. With the exception of few times, it seems that Sun is about to enter the atmosphere here'.

He looked up at the sky, Sun was there. It looked closer than its regular position. *Maybe the end will come by the wrath of Sun. It looks like Sun will burn life on Earth.*

*****

Jim reached for Marshal's house. Busy in a case, like any detective would be, Marshal wasn't answering Jim's phone call. Luckily for him, he had got Marshal that luxurious duplex of which he had secondary keys.

Later that evening, Jim sat alone in his favourite recliner at one side of the ground hall. Power failure had hit that region too which was unexpected. It never happened in a long history. Through the window by his side, rays of moonlight gradually entered a small portion of the space. Even though it comforted him, fear and anxiety rose and fell as he kept thinking about the quest. The objects of the hall were visible by a very dim light coming from three candles from a set of 12; the remaining wax candles were all extinguished. This was a different night for him. He went into a world of deep thinking.

What will the quest unfold now? What mystery lies behind the manifestation of planets? What kind of a race will I be in?

Questions didn't really help elevate his mood for he got no answers. He thought it would, only to realize that thinking raised more questions. The evening relentlessly reminded him of the mystery behind the seven sins he solved last year. He started imagining the human forms of planets; of how they would be like in this day and age. Only he couldn't. Apprehension had killed his imagination.

I suppose, I must get myself out of this state and let time reveal things. He struggled for a moment with the logic that his mind presented him. He got up rather unwillingly; his reasoning gained control over his imagination and made him do it. The light came back. The showy chandelier glittered the entire hall under its effect. He turned to see Marshal by the door.

'Hey Jim, I'm sorry was stuck in an illegal arms deal case', he spoke as he came near Jim. They hugged each other. 'Kathryn told me you were really worried about something and she couldn't tell what over the phone'.

Watching Marshal by his side, for the first time in many hours of that day, he felt some comfort. 'It is so good to see you Marshal', said Jim. 'I guess you'd be aware of what happened today'.

'Yeah, don't tell me about it. Whoever did it made sure that even the secret services don't get wind of the origin of that electro-magnetic pulse. They have managed to maintain secrecy and let the intelligent class of the world speculate. I know they're all clueless at the moment and they can hope at best that this thing remains motionless at least for some time now. Good thing is there hasn't been a loss of life or damage of property'.

'I was in one of the many flights that were affected. Felt like this was my last day when the plane almost fell from the sky. This thing has been set into motion—'

'I can only imagine how terrible it had been for you. I hope you're feeling better now'.

'I am. Feels safe to have feet on the ground'.

'Tell me what's been bothering you?' His words snapped him a little out of his worrisome thinking, albeit not entirely. He was still under anxiety; it hadn't left him from its grasp. Thoughts of how he should share the events with him started throwing itself in every corner of his mind. He quickly decided to tell him everything.

'Marshal!' he uttered. 'I met him'.

'Met who?' Jim fell silent after Marshal questioned. Judging by the look on his face, Marshal gathered there could only be one who would leave such an impact on Jim. 'Don't tell me you met God'.

'Yes I did'.

'Are you sure your mind's not playing tricks on you? It could be a hallucination brought on by lack of sleep. You're sleeping properly, are you?'

'I am, except for the same nightmares that I get. I am serious, I met him'.

'That's great isn't it? How long has it been, a year now?' He seemed positive about it now but Jim had something else in mind. He went near the dining table and saw a reflection of his face on it; signs of fear became obvious to him. He turned to him and spoke, 'You won't like what I'm about to tell you...'

*****

'What happened today is undoubtedly the doing of a planet or planets. He has another quest for you', Marshal got up from his chair after Jim told him everything.

'I need your help Marshal. I need to find the planets. But I don't see a clue that would lead me to them'.

Marshal turned away from Jim. He felt the gravity of the situation sweeping him from his feet. 'This one will be the most difficult case I would be on', he said to himself. He was a wise man and a great friend. He knew that Jim required support in such a time, so he said something that he badly needed to hear— 'I am with you Jim in this. Don't you feel alone my friend'.

Jim got up. 'I don't know what would I do without you'. He paused, looking down at the floor. Anxiety settled down to a great extent after his words though uncertainty still remained. A moment later, they heard a noise of footsteps coming from the other side of the door. Marshal wasn't expecting anyone to come that late. He motioned for Jim to hide behind the table. A doubt sat on him. 'Something's not right. Nobody should come at this hour', thought Marshal. He swiftly took out his gun and positioned himself behind the door. No one knocked the door from the other side. Jim's eyes were so sharp that they caught the view of Marshal turning the door knob. He opened the door quickly and raised his gun at the unexpected visitor.

There was a man at the door. He immediately shot his hands up at Marshal's maneuver.

'Oh it is you Carlyle', Marshal lowered the gun and put it back to its place. 'It's okay Jim, it's just a junior', he said half turning back at Jim. He came out of his cover. Marshal asked, 'What're you doing so late at night?'

'Here's the information you asked for sir', Carlyle took out an envelope and gave it to Marshal.

'You did a great job kid. Next time call before you come'. He closed the door quickly and with his eyes on the envelope, he turned to Jim. 'Whatever you have told me, is startling. Without a clue or a direction, uncertainty would naturally weigh on your spirits'.

'I do not know where to start looking for them'.

'There's a case I am on. It is about an ex-military soldier, or so we know. We didn't have photographs or information but last week I had a tip on the fellow. There's a man named Jameson, he runs an underworld fight club'. Marshal opened the envelop and took out the contents. There were a few papers and pictures.

'And you let him run it?'

'The guy helps the department in homicidal cases. He's more of an asset to us than a liability'.

'He's still doing illegal stuff'.

'There has been not a single death around here under my watch. So I was telling you, he runs a tournament called Bloodsport. Remember the movie? Jean Claud Van Damme?'

'Yeah, I do. Go on'.

'This tournament happens once every quarter with many millionaires, sports enthusiasts, gamblers all bidding for a winner. He takes a good cut, pays us sometimes, under the table of course and stays out of our way'.

'So what about the tournament?'

'The tip was that this ex-military man is under the control of Jameson. He didn't reveal it to me. So I had junior do the digging and get me a proof'. He placed three pictures on the table. 'This is Jameson, the black bald guy. That's the ring I am talking about. And the last picture…'.

Jim looked closely, 'It is unclear'.

'That's him, the guy I am talking about. He has emerged as the top contender of this quarter's tournament. He has been making big money for Jameson. We can track him when he steps out of the ring'.

'Why do you want him so bad?'

'Cause the guy takes law in his own hand. Like a vigilante hell bent on curbing crime. Take note of the crime rates here', Marshal held out one paper he was carrying and pointed to a graph of number of crimes registered in the zone. 'The last year has seen a sudden drop in the crime rate after our superhero emerged out of nowhere. He beats criminals to a pulp before we bring them to justice'.

'Isn't he doing the right thing?'

'Well he is, but there's law and I want to keep it strong. But here is the part that's really strange. Four months ago, one criminal with the name Daniel Patterson was on our wanted list. He was a trained killer. He was suspected to arrive at a certain place where he was going to kill a rich man. We got there to stop him but we reached late'.

'So he killed the rich guy?'

'No. Somebody killed Patterson. When we got there we found him lying dead on that crime scene. We didn't see any marks of beating or torture, not even a scratch. The guy wasn't touched by the person who killed him. We studied everything along with the department's doctor and I found out that right before he was going to kill his target, he suffered an extreme blood pressure level. Have you ever heard of something like it?'

Jim shook his head. 'A criminal dying because of high blood pressure? Never heard of that before'.

'We got his reports. There were no signs of drugs, or an injection, no manhandling. We interrogated the rich man who was targeted. The man said that this dark figure cloaked in dark clothes suddenly emerged from somewhere before Patterson was going to shoot him. Patterson turned his gun to this figure and when he looked at him, his blood boiled, I mean literally'.

'His blood boiled? I get the high blood pressure thing but it boiled?'

'Yes. We had him tested. He wasn't lying. One more case emerged the following week where a gang of five young boys were planning to rob a departmental store. They were successful. We saw the tape of the store. When they exited the camera range, their car stopped. Someone had blocked their way. They got out to beat this imbecile who stood in their way'.

'Was it the same man?'

'We suspect that. The surprising thing is that they didn't attack him', Marshal took a pause as the peculiarity of the case scaled up his mind. 'They started attacking each other'.

'This can't be real. It sounds like a story out of a comic book'.

'I'm telling you the truth Jim. We had them tested and interrogated too. I personally squeezed out the truth from them. All of them said the same thing'.

'What?'

'Right when they got out of their car with the baseball bats in their hands; before they struck that person blocking their way, they felt a surge in anger. It was so immense for each other that they started taking swings at the next man they saw'.

'I don't get it. Were they being hypnotised or what?'

'I can't say because I do not know'.

'How did you establish the connection of this mystery man with the ex-military one who's participating in the tournament?'

'My informer went to that underground battle. He saw everything there. When he gave me the tip, I sensed a strange lowness in his voice when he said—*I haven't seen a human fight like that. There's something unearthly about this fighter'*.

Jim's mind rolled a thought. 'Could it mean that…'

'If a planet has manifested into a human being, it should be him'.

Chapter 4

A voice had been telling Jim something. He could not figure whose it was. *Find them, unite them.*

The illegitimate ring was temporarily organised deep inside the heart of town. It was close to the police department but no one there would look right under their nose for crime. Jameson's timely royalty reached the senior officers including Marshal, keeping their eyes away from most of his actions.

'Are they going to let us enter just like that?' asked Jim. He looked at Marshal's face. The look of a man who had command over everything in the city reflected. Feeling that Marshal had mastered every trick in the book to get things done at his will, Jim caught a breath. Marshal was quiet for a moment and then he answered, 'Entry's convenient for us. Not so convenient for others'.

They passed a taped black line under a gate-arch and reached dead end. A narrow door at the wall was guarded by two huge bouncers who barred the way. Jim noticed guns on them. Both were wearing a tight fitting black t-shirt and trouser. Marshal went up to them, proud and serious. As he spoke to the guards, Jim became aware that he was being discussed. He gazed at them and saw how closely they resembled each other. *Twins.* One guard looked at the other and turned. That was the signal.

'Come, let's go. We're a bit late', said Marshal. The man led them inside. The passage was narrow and uncomfortable for more than two persons to walk at a time. It wasn't long before a clamour was heard in the stairs leading down to the underground ring. There was much cheering and crying of the names of fighters. All show names.

Lessening the distance between the two, Marshal whispered to Jim. 'Don't talk directly to Jameson. We have to be very cunning around that fox. He will veil all his dirty work under a very kind manner. That is how he will present himself, like a clean man'. As they walked downward into the unending spiraling set of stairs, the passage became somewhat darker and what followed was a reddish light reaching the last of the steps. There were multiple shadows of men darkening the radiance. Jim saw torches and their flickering flames light up the bloodsport entrance. Upon entrance, there they saw men and women, ostentatiously dressed to witness blood bath of fighters. There was shaking of hands, small talks. The guard left the two inside. The sight they received next was of a man pummeling another man inside a cage and beating the life out of him. It was a nasty sight for Jim alone.

He looked at the ring. Built with great labour, his men made it high and strong and the business was only flourishing. Jameson was a connected man and many worked for him. Jim couldn't bear the brutality of the place.

'I don't understand how you let these things flourish here'.

'Jameson and others like him have vested their interests here for a year now. If we stop this, they will go back to drugs, trafficking, kidnapping, robbery and killing. I can live with a few people getting killed under my watch. I cannot live watching that number shoot up. You must understand, Jameson has men who follow him; men who would give away their life for him. Because he gives them their livelihood'.

'Out of wrongdoings'.

'It doesn't matter for them. What matters is they don't have empty stomachs at the end of the day. It is best that we don't steer his attention somewhere where the body count would increase'.

Jim didn't speak further. He knew now why Marshal had left these underground battles untouched. It was a simple choice made by people who didn't have control over everything- Save as many as you can and overlook the few who suffer. That was the understanding Jim had framed in his mind.

'There he is', said Marshal. He caught the man, catching his demeanour somewhere in the crowd and his strange voice in the clamour of the closed space. Jim turned and looked straight ahead. A black guy with an awful big cigar in his mouth came and shook hand with another man. He kept hold of his elbow and said, 'This won't be an easy win Jameson'.

Jameson was a white man, bald, stout with a noticeable paunch. He smirked first then replied, 'I would strongly advise you to prepare my bag full of money. I like it heavy'.

'Oh you're so confident tonight. Wait till you see my fighters'. Apparently the two were bidding for the next fight about to happen. It had their men fighting against each other for the pleasure of the spectators. They didn't say much afterwards. There was only an exchange of cocky smiles.

'The bald one?' Jim asked. Marshal nodded and stepped ahead. They went straight to Jameson.

Marshal was the last person Jameson was expecting that night. Furthermore, he had brought a friend with him. He turned to him with a rather calm look. 'There's much to say and do officer, but as you can see I am occupied at the moment. Didn't the bag reach your office?'

'Yes it did'.

'Ah! Then I believe you took the wrong turn and ended up here'. He looked at Jim and not recognising him he asked, 'Who's the gentleman?'

Marshal stepped to his side and spoke, 'He came with me. We're interested in the main event'.

Jameson clearly sensed that they were there for his main man. The bouncers around the place pressed forward towards Jim and Marshal. Jameson motioned his hand from his torso. They stopped and went back to their positions. He didn't want the peace treaty between him and the police to burn that night. Not taking too long, he spoke 'Okay then we must not waste much time. The fight's starting any minute. Join me, I have the VIP box'. He turned and started walking.

Jim looked at Marshal. He got a nod and then they followed him. Jameson led them for a small length to his private box, right above the hexagonal cage. There, deep seats were set about a large glass that faced the cage directly. Two young girl servers, hardly noticed, were standing at the corner of the place with a tray each of drinks. They didn't have clothes about them. Only a limited length of rope barely covered their private parts. They sat after Jameson at the seats which sagged under their weight. The girls brought them wine. Jameson took a glass but the two declined. Jim looked at the heavy make-up of the girls. Under the layer was a grave face made weary of the duty the girl had to carry for her master. Jim's fist became tight and he immediately looked at Marshal.

Marshal shook his head, feeling the pressure that a saddened and angry Jim was going through. He held his hand, trying to appease him. A sudden blaze of yellow-red fire around the ring set ablaze. Their sight shifted to it and they wondered into what gruesome underworld championship was taking place.

Jim heard the voice again in his head. *Find him, convince him.* He didn't understand whose voice was reaching him. Their search for a fighter with wartime service brought them there. He was only hoping to get at least one answer of so many questions he had. Suddenly, his heart moved in a way he hadn't known before. *He's here, I can feel him.*

Cheering rose around the ring. The place was immediately filled with menacing voices of spectators. The main event had begun. And out of the darkness of a chamber under the VIP box, emerged the champion. Jim's eyes fell on the figure that appeared quickly with a brisk stride. He had ample of scars on his back. Jim saw more on his chest when he turned around. Looking at them, it seemed to Marshal that this was the man he was looking for and Jim felt he was none other than the manifestation of a planet. Men wilted with fear upon his daring demeanor and scary look.

'Just look at him. He has been in more battles than anyone would care to count. That's my champion'.

Jim saw him advance towards the cage. He had the look in his eyes—part focused and part rage. 'What do you call him?' Jim asked.

Jameson looked at Jim first, then at Marshal. 'At least we don't have an air of formality here'.

'I know he's from the military', said Marshal.

'He never tells his name. He does what he's told to do. Military or not detective, he works for me now'.

'He should have a name', pressed Jim.

'If you want to know what the people call him, then listen—'. Hagen, Hagen, the crowd began to chant the name in chorus. It only grew in strength and it was understood, he was the favourite underground. But on the ground above them, none had known about him. 'He's called John Hagen. Got that from his badge where we found him'.

'So he is military', Marshal looked sharply at Jameson at this point.

'Loosen up detective, the show's going to start. This is a fight you won't want to miss. I hope you know that we do mixed martial arts here. All's fair inside the ring'.

'But no one dies!'

'Yes that was the deal. No one dies. But the deal's signed between us, not the fighters. I hope you won't mind if somebody gets carried away'. From the other side of the cage, entered three men, who looked bulky, strong and menacing. The trio of mixed martial artists faced John Hagen. The crowd had yet not ceased to chant his name. The trio, it seemed, was facing a hostile crowd.

'That's three against one. It's not a fair fight', said Marshal.

'Yeah! I pity the three', said Jameson.

'You what?' The response didn't go down well for him.

'Do you see fear on his face? Men who can stand like that in front of highly trained fighters are either out of their mind or they know what they are up against'.

The fight began. And as it did, their eyes widened. '*What the…! He's a monster*'. Marshal's breath was stuck; what he witnessed was frightening. John Hagen was breaking bodies. Jim didn't say anything. He was both scared and fascinated, watching Hagen in action. It didn't take too long for Hagen to crush two out of three. Now he had his eyes on the third. Meanwhile, Jameson could feel a great flow of money on him.

'How did you get him? Who is he?' asked Jim. His attention diverted to Jameson. He was accustomed to watching gruesome sights.

Jameson had his eyes glued to the fight but he spoke, 'This guy had been a soldier serving the nation against undisclosed war in Iran. Maybe the guy had an exhibition match you know, the friendly kind they have for entertainment. I guess he got carried away and beat a fellow soldier to a pulp and got thrown out'. Hagen began pounding the third.

'No games. Tell us the truth', pressed Jim. At that, Jim sat up and gripped the arms of the chair. Next his anxiety had taken his body ahead of his seat. Marshal became aware that Jim's hands were trembling with fear and anger as they clutched the armrests. Inside the ring, the third fighter was knocked out cold. A kick to the chin overwhelmed him. All he could do was fall. He couldn't even attempt taking a breath, surrender or tap out for it was Hagen he was up against.

Jameson got up, ecstatic. He turned to Marshal and stretched his hand to his left. One girl immediately put a glass full of wine in it. He finished it all in one go and handed the glass back to the girl. 'If you both want to know so badly, you can meet him in his room. I'll tell my men to take you there'.

Chapter 5

'There's no one in the room', said Jim.

Marshal looked up at the hanging bulb that was nicely illuminating their side of the locker room. He touched it. It was only a little warm. 'He's here'.

'I wish for no stranger here at this time', a voice came from the other side of the lockers. The two went to the side of the voice. Hagen hadn't turned; he was working on his bag and trying to appear indifferent to their presence but a spot of bother appeared in his tone.

'We are not strangers', said Jim. Hagen looked at the two. Seeing their slim bodies, he went back to packing his bag at the locker. 'You don't look like a competitor who can stand inside the ring with me'.

'Valour cannot be computed with only physique. The will to fight for what really matters shows bravery'.

He turned around, furious. 'What do you know about valour, writer? You did not partake in a single battle or peril in your life to call yourself brave'. Just as he finished, the bulb in their section of the locker blasted and the light vanished in a shower of red sparks.

'So, he does know you', said Marshal facing Jim for once, appearing casual yet defensive in his stance.

Jim stepped ahead, 'We met last year, under different circumstance'.

'Your quest brought you to me', Mars said dubiously and smirked. 'There is no quest now. Do not waste my time. I am not what I was. I am a mere insect now'.

'That's how he looks at us humans, like we are insects', Marshal complained to Jim in a tone only he could hear.

'We can't imagine his dread of losing his existence as a planet and coming to a mortal life form'.

'I was going to leave this place tonight. I don't know what made me stay here for two more minutes and listen to you'.

'You're wrong. There is a quest. We need your help to find the others'.

'What makes you think that I'd be interested? I have a life now and I will live the way I desire.'

'You call running like a fugitive a life? Even though you live the life of a vigilante who rids the town of crooks, you serve Jameson'.

'Say no further. You know nothing'.

'I know you. Your loyalty will never leave the man who saved you from treachery of the army. You are the great

Mars I met in the chamber of planets'. Whatever he was saying was aggravating him. The all-powerful Mars was reduced to the body of a human; Jim was unintentionally reminding him of the grave fact.

'Please, we are trying to understand things. We witnessed an unprecedented threat of a mass level today. Jim almost died in plane crash. We believe you can help us. We're trying to do the right thing. We need to know how you became a human?' asked Marshal, attempting to engage him in a conversation before he would make them his punching bag.

'This does not concern you. You are no one to ask anything from me. I will do what I want'.

'Every life has a purpose', spoke Jim. 'Your manifestation could only mean that something great is about to happen. Look if you're not willing to help us, at least come with us, there's nothing for you in here'.

'Something great is about to happen you say; look at me', he turned; the scars all over his body looked deeper when seen from up close. 'Does this look to you as something great—a planet stuck in a human form? I do not want this weak body'.

'Don't make your life seem useless and petty. It is God's will. Why don't you trust it?'

'Because he doesn't trust us anyone. Now leave'. For the most part he had looked at Jim but now he looked at both their faces. 'Leave now and let me remain a slave. If that is the will of God'.

Jim felt taken aback. *He doesn't trust you anymore!What could have happened between God and the planets? I must know. I must convince him.*

'Even I detest that it was Jameson who saved you from a conspiracy. Now he commands your loyalty but we can see that he has you in his hand as nothing more than a pawn. Your place does not lie here and you know it. That is why you go out there and save the innocent. You protect who cannot protect themselves. Ashamed of your body you do it in a clock that covers you. I will not accept you living like this. But tell me before I do anything—what would you do if you were set free?' asked Jim.

Hagen took a moment before he responded. 'My hands are tied by my own word of loyalty to the man who came to me when all turned against me. I refuse freedom as a freely given gift. But it is only freedom I need to make him pay for his deeds. The man walks freely under the nose of the law. He is the conjurer of evil on this Earth, one who has committed innumerable terrible crimes. The detective or his department will not bring Jameson to justice. But I will. I will kill them all if I am set free'.

The air of the room was still. At last when he said that, it became clear to Jim what he was supposed to do next. Marshal didn't like the look of Jim's face. He knew that Jim was going to go to Jameson next and what he was going to do there was beyond his control. He wanted to say 'No' to him but his voice deadened before he opened his mouth and he saw Jim turn and take the door decisively.

'I will not let you stay a slave. The world needs you back in your planetary form. Without you, the world's balance will be shaken'. With that said, he left the room and Marshal with him. The two paced the floor to reach Jameson's room. Haste was needed as Jameson was about to leave. Mars stood at his spot. The straightforward talk of Jim Morgan, his tone of righteous and speed of action made him ponder—*a human coming to the aid of a planet for a selfless purpose.* After so long, the light of freedom dawned in his mind; he could feel destiny's hammer, beating on his chains of servitude; he was imagining lighter hands and they were trying to reach out to freedom in his mind.

Jim and Marshal had entered the private box together.

'I gather that your meeting with my champion didn't go too well', said Jameson. His hands were caressing the brown leather bag and he was relishing the feel of green currency inside it.

'We're here to do business!' spoke Jim. It would take more than words of business to divert Jameson's attention. Nothing mattered more to him than money and he made a hell lot that night. 'We want him'.

He kept his eyes there as he spoke, 'I don't know why I feel to answer a question you asked earlier—about him. Maybe it's the generous man inside me that wants to cooperate or maybe I am in a fantastic mood. Oh well, you wanted to know about my champion'. Finally, he let the bag on his table but he didn't stand too far from it. 'Outside my world, Hagen is yesterday's news. In an instant he was thrown out of the army, humiliated because of the reason I mentioned earlier. A fighter he was and a fighter he remained still. And every fighter needs some action. It wasn't long when he carried an off-the-record assignment for someone. He had been tasked to capture an international terrorist. It was a conspiracy and to his dismay, the operation actually was to eliminate a skilled asset that he was. You know people, they can't stand that someone so skilled is living who can ruin their plans in the future if hired by enemies. So they sent for the paid-killers. He was skilled I tell you, so skilled that once they attacked him from behind, he was able to react and kill everyone. It must be destiny that God had sent me to be there, right after it happened. When I found him, I saw him unconscious with several bullets in his body'. He was looking at the ring from the glass all the while he was telling. He was imagining every detail of it.

'Destiny you say', mocked Jim.

He turned, looking strongly convinced. 'Yes destiny. Have you seen a man swearing an oath to another man and living by it? I have. I only saved him because of his skills, thinking he would make me a few bucks for a favor. But he made me a fortune and look, I am back into business. My order is his command and he will follow it till his last breath'.

'Give me a break. He fights crime, I know it all. Don't tell me Jameson that you command him to do it', said Marshal.

'You don't know me, detective; I am a very generous man. After his battle inside the ring, he disappears into his life of seclusion. I do not interfere there. No one from the outside remembers him. Nobody sends a mail or a message to him. He's invisible on the face of the planet right now. I show him care by giving him the limited freedom he should have. Which brings me to start asking you now—why are you so curious about him?'

It was Jim who answered. 'I think more than "Why I am interested in him", you'd be interested in "How much I am willing to pay for him". Name his price'. Jim had figured in the small time he observed him that only money would make sense to him.

Jameson's eyes flashed suddenly, sensing a fast buck making opportunity. His appetite for money overpowered him and he quickly presented his deal. 'I like your style Mister. So direct and ready to take what you want. But I won't give up my fighter. He's making me big money. Why should I sell my golden goose?'

'How does ten sound to you?'

'Ten million!' Jameson's eyes popped out instantly. He wasn't anticipating Marshal's friend to have that kind of money on him. He was making good money but it would take him a few years with the unground battles and Hagen to make that large a sum. *If he's ready with a ten million in an instant, I can pull him up to a twenty.* The cunning fox in his mind came to life, noticing that it was a rare opportunity to strike.

'If it had been someone else, you would go out empty handed. But it is me that you wish to deal with and the detective knows how generous I am'. He quickly changed his tone from flattering to sharp. 'He's all yours for a twenty'.

'You're insane Jameson', said Marshal.

'It is just business detective. I could have said no on your face. But I didn't say that now, did I? If you want him that bad, I'd say you take the offer', he turned to Jim. 'Take it or leave it'. Marshal looked at the two. It seemed their glances were like blades from eye to eye.

'Deal!' Jim pushed in. 'Money's in the car. Tell your man to get it. I will be waiting for him out there'. Jim went to the door and Marshal could only wonder in surprise. All of this was happening to fast for him. 'And one thing; you're a generous man. Tell Hagen he's free'. Before Jameson could speak further, he left the room and Marshal immediately followed. He was pacing to the car.

Jameson pressed a switch under his table. Two armed men came inside. 'Follow the two and if they don't give the money, shoot them. It is time I say goodbye to my golden goose'.

Chapter 6

'People who blindly follow law think they are above us. They believe they have the power to crush us, direct us when they feel convenient. It was because of them my family, my men starved night after night with no hope of a better future. They were hopelessly dependent on me'. It was the first time Jameson had been opening up before Mars, whom he called John Hagen. To his great shock, which was about to come to him immediately after he sets him free, this was also his last time. 'I never wanted to get into drugs or do the illegal stuff, you know that I have only been a victim of circumstances. I was in search of an answer, I was looking for a way I could feed my people. Then I found you. You were in a mess and my generosity pushed me to take you in. I was lucky, that you became the solution to all my problems. Only because of you I stand today at a place I deserve. And believe me, it is not an overstatement'. He was speaking more and more rapidly now and striding about the room. 'There was a time I was a petty criminal, one who had to elude getting capture. Today I am self-sufficient, today no law enforcer tells me what to do; it is I who tells them to stay at bay and they comply. It is at this moment that I am considered a powerful man; a man who is feared and respected'. Mars's temper was rising with every word he heard. It made him feel responsible. 'And I will not be a self-centered fool. I am what I am because of you. Because of you, I can now feed my people. I can give them shelter, reasons to live and I will forever stay grateful to you for all the tournaments you have fought for me. I am here now as a generous man. I know that you deserve a life better than this', he stretched his hands and looked around the room. 'With a painful heart, I must release you from my protection. I never wanted you to go an inch away from the bond we share but I have decided, for your better future, I will swallow this pill of pain and let you go'.

Jameson's persistent habit of sugar coating his words was infuriating Mars but he kept it boiling only on the inside. He was patient, eager for the moment which would give him the words that would release him of his cuffs. And they were nearest to him now. 'Forgive me if there had been less than perfect care for you on any account', he added defensively. 'At last let me show you my gratitude for all the things that you have done for me', he bowed just a little. For that moment Jameson's eyes glowed as they visioned twenty million which he thought would be waiting in his private box.

'You are free my champion'.

And at that Mars grabbed his neck and closed his eyes forever. The temper was so intense in him; he didn't even want to hear Jameson beg for mercy. Straight away he executed a criminal.

Outside there was starless blackness. Jim and Marshal had almost reached their car followed by two men. The bouncers at the gate were relieved of their duty and they went downstairs for signing out. In haste, they forgot to close the door. It was half open.

'I never saw you put money in the car', said Marshal. He was worried thinking about the consequence of Jim's lie and the result of it on the agreement between the police and Jameson.

'It should happen any second now', Jim didn't even look at him as he said.

'What?' A few seconds later the sound of gunfire from the passage first turned the attention of the guards from them. Then they turned. Mars was raging hell on the family of criminals. As the sound grew, the worse thing to follow was about to come to two men. One of them trembled fearing a dreadful event underground.

'Wait here! I'll check what's happening. You keep an eye on the two', he said with a sense of dawning horror.

'Hmm', he turned to Jim and Marshal. 'You two, don't try anything silly that will cost your life'. He had now a gun pointed at them, just in case. His partner had gone down there for some three minutes now. The sounds were changing, sometimes increasing, sometimes slowing. At the fifth minute, gunshots ceased to make noise. The guard took his instrument, 'Roger, you there? Roger, what's all that noise down there? Roger—' there came no voice from his handset. The terrifying imagination of death on the other side of the door made him feel quite faint. He started trembling but the grip on his gun became tighter, out of fear obviously.

'I suggest you drop the gun and run away', Marshal told the guard.

'Don't say a word more. Oh! What's happening down there? Why isn't Roger responding?'

The door opened slowly and made a screech. He turned reflexively and raised the gun at it. Mars had climbed the last step and came out from it. The guard's eyebrows shot up. There was an immediate impression of death heading his way.

'I am warning you, I'll shoot if you take one step further'. For a person who had dealt with trained assassins, multiple men with machine guns downstairs, giving a warning was equal to giving life away. He had his bag in his hand and began striding at a regular pace.

'Hey, I said—', before the guard could react, Marshal smashed his head with a gun of his own. The impact was strong enough to render him unconscious on the spot. He fell. Marshal poked the gun back inside his jacket. They were quickly joined by Mars. He was so swift that many of Jameson's thugs could not even put up a real fight. But only he knew that. Jim and Marshal could only imagine.

'I'll call Carlyle, tell him to tell the department that he got an anonymous tip about the masked vigilante. They'll see the town getting rid of its dirt. The body count shout be over ten'.

'Twenty three', said Mars immediately.

Marshal took a second to absorb that. 'And you said it is a weak body'. He was walking past Jim now. Jim took two steps towards him and then stopped. He felt that Mars won't cooperate. His head bent in disappointment. But Mars stopped.

'I knew that it was impossible but it happened anyway', he said. Jim looked up and saw him facing him. 'We became humans and some of our powers were transferred in our bodies. I do not fully understand why? But at this point the answer is irrelevant. What's important is that what happened, happened for a reason. Afterwards I knew what I was supposed to do, lead the life of a soldier but I didn't; I couldn't. I was compelled by circumstances to choose to lead a life like this; compelled to suffer. Now I stand here because of you Jim Morgan; because of you I have changed, I am no longer a planet, I am a mere human apparently free like you; free from the bounds of a planetary responsibility. But yet again I am stolen of my choice to live free because I am a supposed to fight with you, not against you'.

'You became human because of him?' questioned Marshal. He was as puzzled as Jim.

'You were right. You have a quest and I have a part in it. That is why I am here'.

Jim was stirred but his impulse brought a stern reply. 'I am not compelling you to be with us. I am requesting you to be help us'.

'You still believe in free will? It is only an illusion. We are here because we have a purpose. Without purpose we would not exist. It is purpose that made me human, it is purpose that has connected us, it is purpose that has pulled you to me and now I am being pulled to your assistance. Your ideology of free will might be guiding you, driving you but wisdom is yet to dawn upon you. Destiny binds us in this quest. Your choices are only the consequences of your fate'.

'I appreciate that you're sharing but I do not and will not share your idea. Marshal don't mind, Mars will always be direct and aggressive. You must know that under the layer of harsh words, there lies a righteous planet'.

'Righteous man now'.

Marshal began noticing that Jim had been acting weirdly. Something was changing him. It concerned him more than the philosophy they were debating. 'I felt something happen to Jim down there. He said and did things sooner than he normally would. Something happened to stir him'.

'You have grown wise, yet with all your subtleties you do not have the wisdom. What you did back in there was you but a power swept you. It was mine'. There was a momentary silence. Mars was now revealing the nature of his power. 'You thought much because all that you wanted to do was set me free. But your thought would remain a thought if I hadn't looked at you with my aspect. Back there I looked at you, and your thought was converted into immediate action. My presence has an effect on people around me. It makes them direct, aggressive and when I saw you, my aspect made you spurt into action'.

'Now I understand', said Jim. 'Planets have aspects. When you look at someone, their body is fed with your energy. But the actions of the person depends on the malice or purity of the heart. Your energy overthrows the mind's thinking with an immediate action'.

Jim looked at Marshal who had his hand over his mouth. He was trying hard to understand a complex phenomenon. 'That explains the boiling of the blood of the hitman and the irrational behaviour of the boys who attacked each other when he looked at them'. He understood the cases that seemed so strange to him; shuddering at his memories as he listened.

Mars continued, 'You must know that there are two follies to avoid. One is that you must maintain a safe distance from malefic planets and the other is that you must avoid my gaze but that is not in your hand'.

'What're Malefics?' posed Marshal.

'Planets like Mars, Saturn are malefic in nature', answered Jim. 'They make us do the less than good things you know. They give us the opposite of what we want'.

'You'll have to elaborate on that'.

'Some other time. Right now you can understand that we consider fighting to be bad. That's the effect of a malefic. What we consider good is the effect of benefic. The presence of benefic like Venus, Jupiter, Moon and Mercury will have a good effect'.

The streetlights began flickering as Mars looked at the two with piercing eyes. They noticed the long alley and the street connecting to it. All the lights even inside curtained apartments were dancing like the flickering street lights.

'It seems clear that our enemy has opened his war on everyone and made the first move', said Mars.

'Now power-issues in a country like America. It seems to me that electricity is where the first blow will fall', said Jim looking at the electricity fluctuation. 'When I was in the plane, a sudden surge of energy fried the plane's systems briefly. We were certain to die in the crash but we were saved; somehow'.

'I didn't ask that earlier, I was too occupied in the case. Later I got to know that everything was alright. Why didn't you call me at the airport? Or when you came to my house?' asked Marshal.

'There was a poor network reception. It came sometimes and sometimes it went off. It has been like this after I landed'.

Mars spoke, 'The time will not be long till there is none. I feel from afar, his haste, his power. Yet I do not know who he is. He is swift and we are yet to understand the entire strategy of our enemy. Only time will tell what doom awaits us and we are not certain how much of it we have. As long as he has his eyes turned that way, you must gather the others. I am sure that the attack will fall on more than just electricity and mobile network. You must meet Moon first. This quest requires you to keep strength. Strength comes from hope. That is what you will find from her'.

'You think she knows something?'

'All of us know something. It is up to you two now, to gather the pieces of this mystery and join them together. Only then will we stand at a position to do anything'.

'But', said Marshal.

'But what? The quest does not allow you for buts tonight'.

'But we don't know where we can find her'.

'I do. Moon is too emotional. God's will and the manifestation left her heart broken. She went off to a desert where she would be alone, maybe with a few special children. I cannot tell you the exact…'

At that moment when Mars was sharing his knowledge of her location, the same voice that had whispered in Jim's ears reached him and blocked all other voices. *Follow the sand. Follow the clouds till you find water in the desert.* It cried faintly and ended.

Marshal was speaking with Mars. 'At this hour, to go to a desert where we don't know we would find her for sure, is madness. We need more specifics of her location'.

Jim turned to him and put his hand on his shoulder. 'We must dare a great risk. It is the need of the hour. Come Marshal, we have a long distance to cover'.

'Go now. I will play my role in your quest'.

Marshal feared that Mars's powers were making Jim rush into things without much thought. And even as they hastened on their way to the car, the wind brought a great deal of clouds and a heavy rain and there arose a feeling of excitement in Marshal. But Jim did not wait. He started the ignition and Mars stood at his spot to see them go ahead on their quest.

Chapter 7

The morning came as a brown dusk; strange it seemed to the two who had been driving for long hours and entered the great desert. Going directionless, guided by a word of Mars and a whisper of an unknown voice, Jim was remembering his wife and daughter. The longing that the husband inside him had, made his heart sank. As the dusk became brighter and day fell upon them, he focused on the quest and forced his heart to be lifted.

'I never drove and looked at the road the way I look at it now', said Jim.

'Yeah you're right. I never marveled the scenery before. It is just the sand, the sun, sky, road and us now. Looking at the desert as it, I feel it is so beautiful'.

'Who knows, tomorrow maybe the whole planet will become a desert, just not as serene as this one'.

'Our world is so fragile, we know so less about the forces— those that work behind the laws of science. It makes me feel all my life's been wasted; knowing that billions of people including me were living oblivious to the existence of planets. I thought I knew a lot about life and the world. Now this happens'.

Jim felt that he ought to start telling Marshal what he thinks and feels about the planets. 'They say that the dinosaurs were wiped from a gigantic meteor or some catastrophic climatic conditions'.

'That's not new to me'.

'Did you know what caused it?'

'Ten hours earlier I wouldn't be able to tell you that. I can put my money on the planets now'.

'Correct'.

'You won't tell me which one?'

'Remind me to ask Mars about it'.

'Don't you find it surprising that God really exists, the planets too are real yet…'

'Yet what?'

'Yet we suffer. I mean there's no one really happy in this world for a long time. It's all temporary. Wouldn't God want to create a world where everyone's happy and living in peace?'

'I guess he'd always wanted that. Our sufferings won't bring him joy. We all come from him. There's a soul in us, an extremely tiny part of the big soul that he is. As best as I know Marshal, eternal happiness is attained when you become one with the source—God. Then there's no attachment with this world which gives you anything less than bliss. You will never find it here. This Earth and this life are just means to reach him'.

'But why didn't God create eternal bliss here? That's my question. Why do you get it only when you become a part of him again?'

'I believe when he created the world, it was perfect. Everyone was happy at first. But as time passed, inside the heart of men breaded envy, wrath, lust, sloth, gluttony, greed and pride. With so many flaws in them, they wouldn't let such bliss exist here. Humans are total disaster in some sense my friend. No one accepted to see anyone else happier, more prosperous than oneself'.

'I wish I had a counter to you but I honestly don't. My experience with the ill men of our society has been so intense that I have to agree with you'.

'You don't have to agree with me. But you can choose to agree with me'.

'What else may have happened then?'

'Man began to enjoy the suffering and misery of another and that gave him pleasure. And hence were born *Asuras* from the sins of man. They gained power from the suffering that one man caused to another. Our hatred, our malice, our sins made them stronger and stronger. But there was compassion and love too that co-existed. They were men who fought for justice, who sacrificed for the greater good. From these emerged the demi-gods that are called *Devtas.* Since time unimaginable they have been governing us'.

'But that is against your explanation of dinosaurs being wiped away from Earth by planets. If these *Devtas* that are the planets came afterwards...'

'No. Let me continue. Dinosaurs and creatures of that time didn't share the same sentiments of a human being. All they knew was hunger, survival and reproduction. With these animal instincts, demi-gods couldn't be born let alone reaching the point of ruling the solar system as planets. Only God and elder planets who were forms of powerful entities lived back then and watched over Earth. With the rise of human species, these *Devtas* and *Asuras* became very powerful. Human beings of that time began to worship the two sides based on their belief set. Moreover, God gave them more powers and with great powers comes great responsibilities. In order to let human civilisation and life progress, the elder planets at that time had to be replaced or you can say the entire system of our galaxy had to be redesigned. But the real question comes here—'

'Replaced by who'

'Precisely. Both sides wanted power. A battle was bought between the *Asuras* and *Devtas* to attain immortality. *Devtas* won it of course, with a great scheme that was made by God himself favouring them. They were then given the role of planets. And under their governance, we thrived'.

'That explains the concept of evolution'.

'Thinking about evolution brings a fear in my mind'.

'Why? What's wrong with evolution?'

'There was a time when dinosaurs had walked this Earth. Today we walk over it. Maybe tomorrow there will be someone else. Maybe we won't be there'.

'Is that the imaginative author speaking?'

'That's the fear that one man of our species has. I wish the future is also our time'.

'Don't know what will happen in that distant a future. We would be long gone to know it'.

'Dinosaurs were a threat to life back then. The way our population is exploding and spreading, our species has already become a threat to life now. If you think like this then you will be convinced that soon enough a planet will throw a meteor at us and wipe us out'.

'Lucky for us, they are humans now'.

'That gives me more fear. If they are here, then who's up there?'

Marshal gave the conversation a pause. 'What happened to the *Asuras* who lost the great battle?'

'So many people have so many theories. But I wish I knew which one was true. I wish I knew'.

Many more hours passed with Marshal at the wheels and Jim taking his break. The day was not yet old and for more hours the journey would go on. The desert was rushing by and the wind that entered through the open window sang loudly in their ears. Jim could see nothing but sand to his right and away to his left the same yellow land as far as his sight could reach. Tired from the long travelling, he tried to remember the good times of his life. His memory was flashing beautiful pictures before him. His intent was bent toward the road ahead, looking out for the place where he would *follow the sand and follow the cloud* as directed by the voice. Yet his mind was still lingering around his daughter who was under the care of his wife.

To Marshal, the quest seemed age long, a directionless journey in a weird dream even though it had not been twenty four hours since he became a part of it. The journey brought with a mist in Jim's eyes of weariness and they closed.

*****

God, standing just before the stretch of a water wave, was looking straight ahead over an ocean. The place appeared as a beach with white sand and blue water; above there was a clear sky. Jim found himself standing a few steps behind him. He thought that God was enjoying the beauty of his creation. Anxious to talk, he joined him. They were now looking straight ahead, observing the wizardry of the endless view. He felt a shiver observing the magnificence. In just a year, he had learnt to enjoy the most of little things that life had to offer. Then he looked at God and noticed that he wasn't wearing a suit. God was in summer casuals, one worn by men who come to beaches for vacations. He had run out of things to say without even opening a talk. What he could say was—

'Why today?'

'It's a good day for conversation'.

'Does it have to begin with questions?'

He smiled, his eyes went down and up on Jim's face. 'It is good to see you Jim'.

His look had a strange way of taking Jim's anxiety away from him and infusing calm. 'It is good to see you too'.

'You want to ask me something. Go ahead'.

'Why're they here, in human form?'

'That's why I am here—to tell you to find that out. Come let's walk and let the air kiss our bodies and take our worries away with it'. He walked first, going past Jim. Then Jim began to walk and catch up with him.

'Fear and uncertainty always bring the first question from you. I wish some other emotion would let you put up a question the next time we meet'.

'I am a victim of circumstance, am I not? They're also a victim of your choice'.

'Now don't make me the devil. I never make choices for anyone. I give them the liberty'.

'Then you didn't make them become humans'.

'You will get to know how it happened. And you already know that their presence and actions are creating an imbalance'.

'Is it only about imbalance?'

'Imbalance is enough to cause more damage than you think'.

'But they're all demi-gods. Right! I mean they are the *Devtas.* They do good'.

'*Devtas* up there do what is to be done. *Devtas* down here, well you can see there's something wrong. You are aware of the nature of the planets. Jupiter, Venus, Moon and Mercury are benefic in nature. While Saturn and Mars are malefic.

'And Sun is mild benefic and mild malefic'.

'Correct'.

'Are you trying to tell me something in particular or is it one of your riddles that you are weaving for me now? I sense that there's something good their manifestation could do. Like they can guide humanity towards peace, prosperity and spirituality too'.

'Their manifestation may even mean human extinction'.

'I could sense an issue of a grand scale but I do not wish to believe that they are behind it. Has someone or something corrupted a planet?'

'I can't tell you'.

Jim wasn't expecting that. Taken aback by a non-cooperative answer, he paused and put forth another question. 'Is a planet in danger?'

'I can't tell you that either'.

'Okay. So you're in a helping mood'. God smiled at his sarcasm. 'Fine. At least tell me who do I search next? After moon I mean…'

'That's a decision you have already made'.

'What! I don't think so'.

'Oh you'll realise it a bit later. All these things happening together are not letting you think straight'.

'Any word of advice?'

'Yes, I got plenty. But for now I will tell you this—what seems true to you might actually be deceiving. What seems plain on the surface will be simmering within. Wisdom, intelligence, hard work, energy, pleasure and emotion will not desert you at a time you need them most. They will be with you. But only light will lead the way'.

Jim looked at the ocean now. 'It always has'.

God smiled. 'It always will'.

He was planning to ask one more question. '*In what far time and place they had come into this world and when would they leave it?*' But before he could, God disappeared.

The ride had been at great speed without a halt and then at late afternoon, Marshal saw a gleam of a big white cloud from the periphery of his right eye. That caught his sight. Far away to the point where the Earth and sky met, he felt white clouds had descended the land. Curiosity led him to turn the wheels. Jim felt a jolt from the sudden turn as Marshal drifted the car away off track to turn to that point.

He looked ahead and the mist before his eyes cleared a little. He rubbed them and now had descended completely into reality from his dream.

Jim said, 'What's the idea?'

'Do you see that?' Marshal's eyes still fixed on that point. 'I think that's where we will follow the sand and the clouds'.

Jim couldn't believe his eyes. 'I can't believe it. It is as if clouds are circling on Earth at that point'.

'Let's go there and find a planet'. The car was blowing away a great amount of sand given the good speed and now they had closed the windows.

Hardly had they reached the place when Jim spoke, 'Do you feel that?'

Marshal felt something. He collected his thoughts and then said, 'It started a while ago, I feel calm and peaceful. The uncertainty of our journey is still with me though'.

'It is the same with me. It is as if our mind is becoming balanced even with the problems that lie ahead of us'.

'We'll definitely find a planet there'.

Jim's irritated mind from the heat of the desert and length of the ride had begun to speak soft words to him. Marshal was dimly aware of the surroundings. His eyes were fixed at the last point of his vision where he saw that white cloud on Earth. After a few miles, a large cloud had just passed over them once again. Jim looked up. It was definitely getting drawn at the point they were heading toward. Marshal reduced the speed of the car when they almost got there.

The noise of the wind became silent. They had come to the silent place where temperature dropped dramatically. The sun shining above the western horizon was gone. Finally, the car slowed to a halt before the standing cloud on Earth. Marshal turned the head lights on to see if daring the car inside the mouth of the cloud works or not. They stepped down from the car and faced the unprecedented place. The lights glowed but couldn't penetrate a feet inside the cloud. It was too dense. Marshal looked down. Moisture had settled around everywhere, he then lifted up his head to contemplate the cause.

Jim saw the shadows of a few birdlike forms. As he looked up, he saw eagles venturing near them, right above their heads. *They are looking at us, surely. But not going inside.* Just as they stepped ahead the mist rolled out. It felt like someone was controlling it; making way for them. The shadows of the predator birds circled away.

'Where are we, Marshal?' Jim asked.

'I wish I had an answer', Marshal spoke. 'If we want to know, we must brave our way in'.

'We're already in', Jim said immediately. The cloud had devoured them. Marshal turned around to check, hc couldn't even see their car. There was silence again for a while as their words fell. Then he spoke, 'We must go'.

It was chilling. Without folded arms across their chests and white smoke coming out of their breaths, they walked up the long winding place. As they did, hope began to kindle in their hearts. They felt as if they would find answers very soon. Striding slowly, they went bounding out of the mist and into entered a green field. It appeared to be a polished garden, with disciplined length of the grass. It was greener than the best gardens of their cities. The trees were thick at the edge of the place with lines of flowers running as bright as sunshine. It looked rich with an orchard.

How in the world can there be such greenery in a land so dry and unfertile. This doesn't look like it is a desert.

The view was unbelievable for the two. Marshal spoke, 'The climate was hot here in Arizona. The weather reported unexpected rainfall in the last week in fixed spots of the desert. It was unnatural. I guess this place and the person conjuring it is the cause of it'.

'That figures! It owes to Moon. Mars was right. That voice I heard was right. She should be here'. Upon entering the vicinity, the air felt pleasantly different. A little cold though but much comfortable than the chill they felt in the barrier of the clouds. Seclusion of any place never felt this welcoming for them.

A few mature women draped in white cloaks were watering plants; one was feeding pigeons, two cuddling small animals and a few others feeding people. They were old, in their fifties or sixties. There dwelt not many and one stood out in the eyes of Jim. She was in white robe, had white hair. Her face looked caring and honest. The wrinkles on her face didn't speak of stress or worry, just good age and experience.

She walked out into the garden with a bowl full of something white. As the two stepped ahead and she leant forward to a row of children, they found her serving rice to a bald boy. Then she moved to the next and to the next till she served them all. There was one thing surprisingly common in them all. They were all bald and slim. A girl came running and hid behind her. She turned to ask, 'What is it dear?'

The little girl looked out from the shelter of her white cloak. 'Who are they, Mother', she cried, clutching at the cloak.

Then her eyes fell on them. There was much of purity in the beautiful blue eyes. Jim became motionless and his mind began capturing emotions of nurture and care she was transferring to him through her gaze. It had a very pleasant and soothing effect about it. They were staring at a sight they hadn't seen before, feeling peace and bliss through waves that came from her eyes.

At length she spoke, 'I figured the turn you would take will get you here. You're here at the right time sons. Dia, go tell the women to prepare the meal I told them for our guests'.

They were far enough to miss what she spoke to her. Before they spoke a word, Jim suddenly remembered that he was very hungry. He looked at Marshal to see if he felt the same.

The woman read his thoughts from the expression on his face. She intently looked to her left letting their eyes follow her sight. There was a table and three chairs, with exactly three plates and water glasses under a wooden shelter that appeared like a hut of some forgotten time.

'How did you know that…?' Marshal couldn't complete his question under the spell of amazement.

She smiled, 'We planets know everybody, every organism. We are in you, we watch you from the inside and also...' She didn't need to look up. They knew she meant from the sky. 'Just for some time now we are amongst you. Come now, we must relish the goodness that God has given us'. A woman took the container from her and she led them.

They walked up a ramp to the hut. A lot of things were being prepared in the kitchen adjoining it. Inside the open kitchen a few women, not as old looking as Moon, were trying to light damp wood. Eventually, the fire caught and two ladies placed a giant container over it. Through the immense chimney that stood large, smoke exited. The two stopped before the table.

'They're preparing dessert for the night', she said. 'Come on, don't be shy'.

A much unexpected cordial treatment would leave anyone in confusion. But her presence and gaze transferred calm in them. They sat. Jim's eyes rolled over the table. There was no dark finger marks or stains of any kind on the white of the table and plates. Three ladies in white robes akin to Moon came over with one container each of food for them. Jim's nostrils caught some smoke from the tray. It appeared piping hot. He could smell aroma of strong masalas. Hungry he was and the eagerness to look him got an unpleasant sight. The meal was very Indian, a cuisine he never liked.

'You won't get to order today boys. The menu is pre-decided'.

'Saves us some energy', said Marshal instantly as if he was sitting at home, comfortable with family he didn't have.

'You'll need lots of energy and wits this time son'.

'This time?' asked Jim, still thinking he had to force the meal down his throat. Another lady brought plates and they were served well.

'Ah! Never mind. Let's just finish this first', said Marshal. He started digging fingers in the mountain of rice and the liquid dressing over it which was like the gravy of a spicy dish. The way he ate wasn't clean, as Jim thought. He was used to fork and knife.

For Marshal, there was no problem with the hospitality or the food. He loved Indian cuisine the most and had been used to eating it the traditional way. All the time, Jim saw Moon enjoying every grain she ate with them. Watching her relish the most out of smallest things was a quality he wished he had.

She looked at him, 'You never learnt compromising in life'.

'This is delicious. Don't wait up or I'll take yours too', Marshal said with a mouthful.

'You are our guest so you won't be disappointed', said Moon. She held her hand over his plate and moved it over the food. Both of them looked at the first move, nothing happened. But with the second one, the food changed into an American cheese burger. They froze, amazed with eyes fixed on the little magic her hand movement showed them.

'Wow! You can change food?' asked Jim.

'Not just change but create as well'. She placed her palm facing up before Marshal's plate and as she very slowly raised it, the mountain of rice grew and the dressing spread over it.

'That's the best magic I've seen in my life. Thank you very much', complimented Marshal. She took her hand back on her plate and continued eating. 'You can eat, it's fresh'.

Jim had the burger on his mouth but curiosity let him ask as we as eat. 'If you can do it with your hand, why prepare food on wood?'

She raised her nose from the food and met his eyes. A smile flitted across her face. 'I was expecting that question from you. We do that for the flavour'. He smiled back. Marshal was occupied eating. 'Magic can surprise you one time maybe two but the same magic doesn't give you the same impact the third time. But preparing food the natural way does that every time'.

There was much to learn from her thought Jim. Everything about her was exceptional. They finished their meal in a short while. Never had they enjoyed food all their life like they did then. A lady from the kitchen came hurrying out. 'Just in time for the dessert'. The lady who served them initially was with them all the time. She cleaned the table and another one laid a few cups before them. A gluey white liquid was poured into the cups. It had a dressing of cashew nuts, almonds and pistachios.

'What's this?' asked Jim.

'It is an Indian sweet. How do you pronounce it Durga,' she turned to the lady.

'It is called Phirni', she said.

'Oh yes, you should try it, it is delicious. Go on, eat till you are satisfied'.

Jim watched this dessert leave curls of vapour. He wasn't sure if his gut would take it nicely or not. It was his first time. First times shocked him more than they surprised him but this time was different. The first spoon full of the dessert was savoury. He looked at Marshal. His face gradually took on an expression of contentment. He neatly rolled his sleeves and put his forearms on the table and looked at her again. The exercise was giving him calm and fulfillment more than his writing passion. The caress of look through her face felt like a mother to him.

'Why this chilly mist in a desert?'

'Isn't it obvious? Nobody comes in a desert. But there are those who have their eyes on the supernatural powers of my gifted children. Some even tried penetrating the barrier and taking what doesn't belong to them. They found the chilly mist instead. It suppressed their communications, failed their machines and arms and blinded them. Men without eyes and no control of senses become harmless. Yet greed forces their feet to dare trespass, still. They were led over a big hole; they fell and never emerged again'.

'That makes us lucky, we didn't drift ourselves there'.

'The mist would have swayed you if your heart was filled with malice. Don't put it on luck, over here, safety lies in your motives. But it isn't your motive we must talk about. I am aware that you bring with you many questions. And I will answer them to your satisfaction'.

'Why are you here? Why are all of you here with us?' Jim asked as Marshal too was now serious.

'Is it not as much our Earth as it is yours?' Her gentle voice had a soothing effect on them.

'No, no that's not what I meant, I'm—'

She laughed out for a few seconds. He checked Marshal not knowing what he said wrong. 'I am sorry, I just wanted to see how you react my son'. She gently patted her palm twice over his cheek. 'Don't mind. I try to talk like young people do; be fun and have fun with children'.

He was still dazed by her behaviour. Some sixteen hours earlier, they confronted the fierce Mars and now the exact opposite. The difference was immense. Marshal smiled, leaned and pressed, gingerly, 'Please share with us', he was about to say madam, but took a pause, rolled back that word and said, 'Mother'.

Moon was pleased with his manners. 'Does it matter? Not that I don't want to tell you, knowing why we are here is not necessary. The question that you should be asking is what are we going to do here?'

'Yes, we would like to ask that as well'.

The smile vanished in a moment from her face. As grave the matter was, it was time she decided to present things on a serious note. 'We have decided to live the life of human beings and taken the form of humans on Earth. But a Malefic Planet maybe even more, is creating chaos or as I feel they are making a Benefic Planet do their dirty work'. Her words put a sense of apprehension in them for the first time since their arrival. She continued, 'The world is about to face a grave situation which might result in complete destruction. You must solve the mystery behind the chaos maker before we break the Balance of the Earth'.

They didn't speak for next couple of seconds. 'In order to solve the mystery, we need your help. We must unite everyone', said Marshal.

'Maybe you shouldn't', she responded. That left him in confusion. 'Jim, why don't you tell him why I said it?'

Jim didn't know what she was talking about. Believing a reason behind her statement, he began pondering. 'Mars told us to stay away from the presence and gaze of malefic planets. It has potential of causing harm to us. If you suggest that we shouldn't unite all of you, I gather that a malefic's presence and gaze can also cause harm to the benefic planets'.

'Your imagination and reasoning never ceases to amaze me dear son. Have you devised a plan yet?'

'I don't have one and I am sure not to make yet. We can't give ourselves a false sense of security with a plan that we don't know will work'.

'Yes', added Marshal. 'Wedon't know who our enemy is, what he is up to. We don't know what he wants now, why is he doing what he's doing, where is they and certainly what he wants next. Mars and you have made it clear to us that it is connected with global disaster'.

'You are pitted against a foe too great. You don't know if your enemy is a he or a she or it'.

'She?' asked Marshal. 'It?' asked Jim.

'If a malefic casted a spell on me through gaze or presence, maybe I would be the enemy you're looking for'. Sensing that she suggested that any planet could be creating the course of disaster for humanity including her made Jim forget his hope in his terror. Noticing it, she immediately said, 'I would suggest you give yourself a little hope with some action'.

'We were told the contrary. Mars told us to find you for hope'.

'Mars is righteous but even he speaks before he thinks'.

'Why are you here, where there is no connection with the world, just these needy people?'

'I can do some good here Jim. There, you might just have to go up against me'. They didn't understand. 'I represent emotions, water, care and nurture. Emotions are most vulnerable. Water takes the shape of its container; care and nurture have the tendency to become subjective'.

Marshal said at this, 'I still don't understand why you stay hidden here'.

Jim answered for him this time. 'Out of all the planets Marshal, it is Moon which gets affected the most. A benefic aspect can be a great blessing and a malefic one might give rise to destruction. She cares for us that is why she is away from us. She doesn't want to add to our woes'.

'You think we can make it? I mean, we're just humans and we're up against planets', said Marshal.

'You must understand one thing. There will come a time when you will find some of us standing with you. But there will be some of us against you. Your journey brought you here to me. I am giving you the wisdom not to take me with you'.

Knowing that she must refrain from uniting with all others, a little despair made its way into their hearts. She looked at them firmly. 'Now you know that you must walk your path without me. This knowledge will be a great strength to you in your quest'. Their hearts arouse with hope again knowing that they knew at least something useful.

Suddenly, the image of the man Jim saw sitting on a green chair in his nightmare flashed before him. The movement of the headless shadow that loomed over the man grew stronger. The strange voice whispered in his ears again. *Find him. Save him.*

He got up in a start. At that moment, he feared it was time for them to leave. He had found what he was looking for—Hope. And it was there to stay with him, at least that is what he felt. He thought parting with Moon wouldn't be easy but she made it memorable, giving two more things along with hope to the two. Faith in their intention and strength in their resolve.

Chapter 8

Jim had heard another whisper after an hour he left Moon. *Seek wisdom, week white cover over land.* Immediately after the whisper, he saw vision of a sage he had seen in his nightmare. He told Marshal to go back to his headquarter, reunite with Mars and try to find the remaining planets by looking into files that tell about extraordinary persons. Marshal's reluctance didn't last long; Jim was able to persuade him. He was dropped at a motel in the middle of nowhere where he was able to get himself a car. Both of them parted in different directions. Jim had a fairly good idea about the white cover that the whisper mentioned to him. It was a mountain range Jim had visited years earlier for leisure. Slowly he passed out of a hot day of hope into the darkness of a starless night, but he still had the resolve which would not let his spirit die.

'Where do you think he'd be?' he remembered Marshal asking him.

'Where everything pure and spiritual resides. The home to transcendence'.

'Somewhere overseas?'

'No. The mountains'.

It was a long day's drive. There was a lodge just a few miles before the mountains. It appeared to be well on the outskirt, pretty conservative and not even a little attractive for tourist. 'God knows when I'll meet this sage or what I'll see', he thought at the threshold. He heaved open the wooden door of the lodge, it was heavy. There was no security guard or a person inside to help him with it. Service was poor. He stepped inside. The air was a couple of degrees warmer but the place was dim with only two of the many fluorescent lamps lit. There came no light from a candle-filled lamp that hung on the ceiling; it was only for showy purpose. The walls were covered by light brown wall papers and they weren't impressive. He found two men sitting inside the lobby on two old armchairs at the near corner. One of them gestured to the other as he saw Jim. He turned and saw a visitor. Glad, he got up in an instant and came rushing behind the reception table. Jim was expected movement of tourists and many servers but as he assessed, there was no sign of occupants; no sound of children coming from the two floors, even outside there was only Jim's car. He was alone. The place had an air of complete neglect and he realised that it wasn't inhabited for a long time now. He stepped up to the table. The receptionist didn't move and kept smiling at Jim.

'Greeting sir', he welcomed Jim, his thin mouth curling into a smile. 'Is it the search of the great mystic that brings you here?'

'Yes, I read about a monk with supernatural powers has made the mountains his home'.

'You came at the right place. Many people come here looking for him. All the occupants vacated this morning after we took them to him and they got his blessings'.

'You know where he is?'

'Yes sir, our main business now is escorting our guests to the saint. When do you want to meet him?'

'Right now if that can be arranged'.

'Very well. Stewart', he called out his partner who got up from his seat. 'Bring sir some warmers, he'll need them. And call Marcus to ready the car'.

'I must say, you're quick'.

'We're always ready, many people come here in search of him'.

'Mind if I ask you your name?'

'Oh! Sorry I didn't introduce myself. I am Kevin', he was holding his hand out.

'Jim', they shook. Please use the restroom and give us ten minutes, we'll have everything ready. The climb will take an hour by car and then we'll go on foot; that'll add another two hours. But I guarantee, it'll be worth the blessings that you will get from him'.

'You too got blessed'.

'Yes sir. We are doing absolutely great. The services will cost you five grand and it will include your safety, food, water and everything else you would not even expect'.

'Five grand! Isn't that too much?'

'After this, I guarantee you'll give me double. The wires are troubling us here, so we cannot assist you in card transfer. I hope cash won't be an issue for you', he said with a little cunning smile and a caress of his right hand on his left.

'If its cash you want, I only have four with me now'.

'Hmm, let me see. It's okay; we can give you a discount for prompt visit'.

Jim took out four from his wallet, not showing the remaining ten grand in cash to Kevin. 'Here you go'.

'Thank you sir. I'll be back in no time; allow me to arrange for you'.

Jim settled himself in one of the armchairs. Within minutes, Stewart came bearing a tray of a glass of water. He then quickly placed it before Jim and in another minute brought him warmers. He looked sincere but his nose was pointed which spoke otherwise. Afterwards he used the restroom and moved to the hall again where Steward and Kevin had been waiting for him.

'Everything's arranged, we can start moving', said Kevin.

They took him outside where a Jeep was releasing a lot of smoke from the exhaust. The driver got out, he looked like he was in middle forties but he looked sharp. The way he lifted heavy bag and placed it inside the boot made it clear that he had been doing this for a good time now. Clean shaven, well dressed, Jim was glad to see a reasonable reception. He was of average height and a little wide. The rest were slim. Jim sat in the rear seat with Stewart; Marcus and Kevin sat in the front.

There was no sign of car movement, not even tracks over the limited snow on the road. Marcus took a path that skirted the foothill for a few miles. After turning several times and crossing a mountain, the view of the lodge disappeared. Cruising through the one lane mountain road, turning by instincts as the fog had limited sight, maneuvering the car's speed for that treacherous road required great skill and experience. Marcus it seemed had all of it. Jim was quiet all the time. With thoughts partly lingering over Leia and Kathryn, he felt the warmth of his blood stolen away by destiny as he had to part away from them for time uncertain. He had heard that landslides were common during this time of the year and was hoping not to witness it. After an hour, Marcus saw neon up ahead shining from the headlight that pierced the morning fog. He pulled the Jeep in off the road, just before the head-high sign saying, 'Dead End'.

'This is as far as the car can go. Kevin will take you ahead from this point', Marcus turned back and said.

'I think it'll be great if we all go', said Jim.

'I think that will be best for us', added Kevin.

Marcus agreed without even the slightest argument. Stewart joined up with them all and they began walking with the heavy utilities on their backs. Jim didn't realise that there was no path; he was being lead from the gaps that prevailed in the density of trees on the mountains. *That sage sure seems to live far away.* Kevin and Marcus had been leading; Jim was pursuing them, and Stewart was pursuing Jim, keeping a distance. They treaded further into the forest.

After just ten minutes, when all was silent and the path seemed to end at a cliff, Kevin stopped just next to Jim. He turned when Jim saw a dead end and he could not get any further. *Something's not right.* He turned to see a large knife in Kevin's hand. It struck Jim that he was brought here under false pretense. A little misdirection was enough to have him there alone.

'What's this for?' Jim asked fearfully.

'For the remaining cash mister. I trust currency here more than the bank', replied Kevin.

'And the cards of course, we can trust the money machines elsewhere', said Stewart. Marcus was silent as usual.

'What do you mean by that?'

'Haven't you been reading? The banks aren't working for a week now around the area. If you're smart you'll not waste my time and do the right thing. Now give me your wallet if you want this to end quickly and nicely'. The range had been facing information issues. Jim immediately understood that banks were beginning to face trouble from internet glitches and the officials would only declare it as an error of server not to scare the public. Something big was already happening around the world. He sensed impending danger; a danger that raged unchecked.

'And the sage story?'

'We made it up. You're not the first who's falling for it', said Stewart.

'Now', shouted Kevin.

Jim hesitated for a moment, thinking he would let his word prowess buy him a way out, but it only existed in the books more than it did in real life. His eye went behind Kevin. 'I can't believe it', he said.

'Don't try to act smart now. Give me…', before he could complete, somebody grabbed his neck and lifted him in the air. Before he could notice, he felt a tight grip on the hand he was holding his knife at and it became tighter till he started screaming. It was Mars. He strengthened his hold and Kevin's body began trembling.

'That's enough', said Jim. He didn't listen. Kevin's knife fell from his hand and he lost consciousness while hanging in Mars's hand. 'Please don't kill him', said Stewart, standing completely motionless, his face covered in fear. Although he was better in built, Marcus had the same. Mars's maneuver would cripple anyone's spirit and send tremor in heart. He released the crushed hand of Kevin that he had held and dropped him from his other hand. Kevin fell.

Mars turned to the two, pointed his hand at Kevin and forced it behind them. They nodded and quickly took the unconscious body and pushed their legs back to the car. Mars was with Jim. His presence added heat to Jim's body.

'Thank you, I didn't expect you to come down...'

'Save it', interrupted Mars. 'I didn't come here for you. I seek Jupiter who has hidden somewhere in these mountains;

it is only chance that I stumbled upon you'. He had already walked past Jim as he said. He was rude on the surface and in his voice but Jim felt the righteousness he bore underneath.

'Why do you try so hard to—?'

'I don't need to answer your petty questions. There is a presence I feel, of a planet. The leaves were right. Come, we must hurry'. Mars pressed his words loudly as Jim showed a sign of asking questions. But Jim was clever, so he reduced his following questions to a few words.

'The leaves?'

'Now look, because of you I have lost my way. I will have to summon them again'. Jim was confused listening to Mars and grew more when he saw him going to the nearest tree.

'*Rasdullopalgorla* Jupiter', Mars said. Jim could only understand Jupiter. It seemed he was speaking a planet's language to the tree. He opened his mouth but Mars forestalled him. 'See what this tree tells us'. The tree began to shake as if it was awaken from a frozen dream. The snow that some of the leaves were covered with, fell. Jim was surprised, amazed to the maximum. The tree shook some more and with most of the snow fell a few leaves on Mars's feet. He picked one brought it near him.

Watching the leaf for ten seconds he spoke, 'Ah! There he is. Can you see him moving?'

'See what, whom?'

'You can't because you don't have a planet's sight. This is one of the few powers that I have. This leaf is showing me that Jupiter once came on this path. There are eleven leaves fallen near my feet, it tells me that he was last here eleven months ago'.

'And if they had fallen on your head?'

'For the first time you asked me a sensible question. If they fall on head, shows minutes. If on hands shows hours, on feet is days, near them is months, away from them is years and if they drop farther it shows decades'.

'These trees can see things?'

'They see everything around them. They're like cameras which record the things they see. Leaves are the memory banks of trees. If a leaf is full with data, they wither or fall and die. The ones which hang are recording what they are seeing now'.

'Well, where's he going?'

'Hard to tell like this; there's snow everywhere. Let me show you how I found this point in the first place. *Peedos* Jupiter', he shouted. Jim felt he meant a hundred trees to hear it. Silence lasted for a few moments.

'What now?' asked Jim, wanting to see marvelous magic of the planet. Mars didn't speak. He simply stepped away from the trees. Jim did the same, fearing something unseen.

The trees began to shake just like the first one. The noise grew from a few trees to many and many more. Snow was falling on the ground but the leaves weren't like the last time. A breeze unlike any other emerged from nowhere and then countess leaves began to fly with it in circles. Jim stepped hear Mars and saw the dance of the leaves. Quickly, one leaf fell on Mars's feet then another fell away a foot away from it followed by many more in the same gaps of a foot. They were making a sort of line that was stretching to a higher mountain range. Within less than a minute, all of them were on the ground and it appeared that a direction was set towards Jupiter.

'They'll take us to him right', Jim's tone was more of a statement than a question. 'Come on let's follow them'.

'Yes indeed', Mars said in a bored way, feeling at loss of a compliment he should have received for showing this to him.

Now I need not worry. His presence will certainly save me from the snows of Alaska. Even with his bodily limitations, he was proving to be a great saviour. Jim was a slow walker on the snow. Mars began to lead him. It was a long way and shortly, Jim was out of breath. The air was heavy, the road was briefly visible under the cloud of moist and his sight couldn't reach the peak of mountains. Gradually, from the forests the leaves led them to a path. It passed from one slope to another. As they walked up, the mist submerged everything around them. They stopped at a point where not even the leaves on the ground were visible. The clouds replaced everything with themselves. There were no more tree shadows like in the initial time of their search. Mars looked ahead, the road was gone. Jim descended a few steps out of uncertainty and saw the cliff vanishing. Even the great mountain that reared its head proudly right to them wasn't visible anymore. Breath flew from their nostrils;

white breath. It was plain white everywhere. The little hope Jim was carrying first sank into nothingness, then it turned into frustration. It had to go that way given Mars's hot presence.

'This is unreal', said Jim.

Mars looked around. 'Yes, I haven't seen anything like it'.

'What should we do now?'

'We walk, slowly'. He heard him. They drew closer to each other—in case either of them fells the cliff, the second man can save the first. At best they could see their legs and the part under their nose. Mars said, 'Do you see something up ahead?' and treaded. Jim lifted his nose to see nothing. His eyes couldn't see much.

'Stop', he said. 'Why do I get the feeling that we're at the exact place where we started at'?

Jim saw the place where Mars thrashed Kevin. The snow had their tracks and the spot where Kevin fell was uneven. 'What's happening?'

'It must have been some time now. We were advancing without a direction, thinking we had one. Come on, we must continue'. Jim didn't know what to say. He wasn't disappointed in the magic of the leaves but he was ruminating about a possible magic that had them get back to their starting point. He walked with a bowed head and Mars with his usual proud head. They kept walking for some time and did not speak. Jim noticed that after treading for the second time, they came back to the exact spot they had started from.

'What is this?' Jim said standing baffled at the place he saw. 'Walking isn't getting us any further'.

'You're right. It seems Jupiter does not want to meet us'.

'Your powers are limited in your body yet it is mind boggling that with incantations you can control nature'.

'And that's going against us at the moment'.

'There's nothing but clouds all around us. I can't even see my feet now. Is there a spell which can disburse this?'

'Yes there is but only the teacher of all knows it'.

'That's just great'.

'See how I will vaporise what blinds us'. His face turned stern and he started throwing his aspect on the clouds. Jim felt the temperature going high shortly. He distanced himself from him. Mars turned his gaze around them and the white of the place started to melt. The fog that was obscuring everything in their sight was turning into liquid and the liquid turned into vapours. Jim's eyes scanned and saw all of it vanishing when suddenly he noticed an unusual opening at the rock that stood large before them. To a great surprise, it wasn't there earlier. Jim moved towards it. Something was pulling him from beyond. As he went near it, a portion of the rock, the size of a ten feet tall animal, started to melt inside the rock and took shape of a door. Mars stepped near it and it disappeared bringing back the old shape of the rock to them. He felt peculiar. Out of instinct, he stepped back and saw the part of the rock form into a door again. Jim looked at Mars, clueless. Mars, with a gesture of head told him to go to it. In the next step of his, the door blew open and a passage appeared.

'It's a cave', said Jim. 'Should we go inside?'

'What awaits you at the other side is only meant for you. Go now, I will wait here'.

'But, if there's danger there...?'

'Do not argue. Do as I say'.

Jim felt that he should follow Mars's instruction. He first looked at it and swallowed his fear and stepped ahead softly. He turned back, Mars was watching him. He walked carefully; the door didn't close when he was inside. The cave was dull but a soothing yellow light, coming from the other end was pulling Jim. He went across the cave and came to a place that appeared like heaven. He looked about the place. The sun was shining warm and bright high in the blue sky. Jim's eyes fell upon the serenity of the garden. He moved and caught sight of someone sitting under the only tree there. It was a man in a yellowish robe. Jim stepped ahead, cautious, not knowing if he was welcome or not. The tree was giving company to this person. It was casting a long and clear cut shadow westward, away from him, not disturbing him as the person appeared in meditation. The plain grey turban and long white hair extending till his neck end accentuated his saint-like look. He was very still, appearing as if in a mode of transcendence.

Jim went to him. It was clear to him that he was expected. He stood looking at the man for a short while, unheeded.

'What are you?'

'Why do you think God gives you the privilege of his company?'

I had been wondering the same for a year now. 'Maybe I have a purpose'.

'Everyone has a purpose'.

'I think I have a significant purpose'.

'Significant over…?' Jim was short of response. 'If you let your importance of yourself go, you will find wisdom. And in wisdom lies your answer'.

Jim now knew that it was Jupiter, the planet of wisdom and prosperity. 'You're the wisest sir. I wish to be enlightened'.

'Enlightenment will come to you but you have to wait. Now we have a more important task'.

'Yes we do. The kind of things happening around worries me. It is like so far I have only scratched the tip of the iceberg. I can't imagine what's underneath the surface. It gives me jitters'.

'I know who's behind all this'.

'Then please tell me'.

'I cannot. My answer will possibly trigger three responses from you. All the three will eventually end up taking you to your demise'. Jim felt a jolt as he heard the word of his likely demise. 'But there's a slight chance you can set things right. For that to happen you have to stay out of knowledge of things'.

'I think I can do better if you tell me about it'.

'He has already impacted you'.

'He what? Who're you talking about?'

'You must analyse your actions to understand this'.

'Quit giving me puzzles already and come straight to the point'. What was I saying? I had never been so direct and thoughtless. He looked at me and saw issues in my eyes.

'Let me enlighten you'. His eyes widened a little looking at me. Almost instantly, he felt what he meant.

Mars's aspect on me had made me aggressive. If I have to get to the end point, I would need Mars's energy and also Jupiter's wisdom. Going out guns blazing would land me in trouble for sure. I need to balance between the two energies. His continuous glare had a tremendous impact on me.

'There's something strange about this place. I feel soothed and calm from the outside, but not from within'.

'It has not been long since you felt my presence. You will feel wiser from now'. He lapsed into the same kind of feeling Jim had felt when he came here. A feeling that he felt during his writing days: happiness from the outside, loneliness from the inside.

'Come and sit with me. Let's breathe wisdom these silent mountains have to offer us'. He sat next to him and felt a little uncomfortable. *He is the teacher of all planets. I am just a human being. Should I be partaking in this insolence?*

'You have questions. I will try to show you the way'. He had a really polite way of communicating.

'If Mars is impacting me, should he be with me all the time?'

'Courage will be your biggest strength against the storm that you will face in this journey. He has a big role to play in this one my child'.

'Even more than you?' Jim said and there followed a moment of silence. 'Won't you join us to stop the enemy planet? We need you if we've to stand against him'.

'Enemy planet you say. Him you say. What makes you so sure that the planet who is an enemy is him?' Jim fell silent on his question. 'I will not fool you with many questions. You do not have time. I will open your eyes. It is Mercury who is behind all this. You must find him and stop him'.

Mercury! How does he know? Why is it him?

A smile flitted across Jupiter's face. 'For the people, my aspect works more than my presence for I come seldom. My aspect will stay with you and it will guide you. If I must come when I am needed the most, I will come. And I must also warn you'.

'Of what? You know of something, though you haven't spoken of earlier'. It was more of a question from Jim than a statement. 'I can sense that you see something treacherous is about to unfold and when it does, all will depend upon me'.

'Hear me well and remember these words—when all options are lost but one, you will have to make a choice between a Benefic and a Malefic'.

'What must I do then to defeat Mercury? I do not even know where he is'.

'Your friend, the detective will tell you where to find him. And when the time comes choose the Benefic planet, for a Malefic will still bring misery on you'.

Jim heard it well and took some time to ask more. 'Is there something else I should know?'

'Leave your dependence on us and sharpen your faith in yourself'. Jupiter shared more with him and ever as Jim listened, he was more amazed with the words of wisdom, and looked at greater wonder at Jupiter.

Mars had waited at the exit of the cave, walking back and forth, impatiently. Such was his nature. When Jim's purpose there was over, he went back to the entrance of the cave where Mars had cleared a line of snow under his continuous movement. Jupiter stayed at his spot and went back into his meditative state. He told Jim that his time had not come to get engaged. When it comes, he'll be with them. Jim was counting on it. He was about to reveal the gist of their conversation to Mars when he was interrupted, 'What he told was told for you alone. When the time comes, you must decide to walk on the path he showed you or not'.

'How do you know that he only gave me a direction and not help in person?'

'Jupiter's a teacher. He teaches; I perform the actions'. With that he began walking back to their lodge from where they would take Jim's car to join Marshal. Jim followed him as usual but Mars took him to some other route. Thinking that it was a faster one, he didn't question.

The sun was now climbing and the fog in the track below was dispersing. The last of it was floating away. Witnessing a drastic change in the sight Jim said, 'It almost feels like it is an illusion, all of this'. Mars thought so. He didn't expect a mirage from Jupiter. Such creation was not in Jupiter's power or aspect as Mars had known him. But it was the work of a spell. Suspicion developed in his mind about the reason why he didn't want him to join him yet he did not give his thoughts the shape of words before Jim.

The thought of a long journey back to Marshal along with Mars this time, made him feel tired already. Mars somehow read from the look on his face and passed a stinging remark, 'You are so naïve'.

'Now what did I do?'

'You think I came all the way here by some human transport'.

He never even realised that they had approached a frozen lake. 'But of course', he stopped his lips anticipating another spell or trick involved which would create a magic route.

Mars was stepping up the lake now. 'The elements have more to them than you can know. Take for instance water. It was used centuries ago by wizards, teachers with magical powers, gurus and sages to reach places on Earth no one had ever seen or heard of. But water is under the command of the moon and in order for this spell to work we need her'.

'But she's—'

'Far away, isn't she? I am not talking about the human body of moon, I am talking about the planet. Look up'.

'It's time for moon to climb, many hours'.

'Look down'.

'I see the reflection of the sun'.

'These incantations are powerful and hence must be known only to us'. He spread his arms around the reflection of the sun on the lake's surface. 'Your friend awaits you', he said looking half back at Jim and then he looked at the reflection again. '*KeidusTrevos* Marshal'.

Jim looked at the sun's reflection. It was turning white from yellow and it became completely circular within seconds and started glowing whiter than the moon. He looked up, there was sun but down on the reflection he saw moon. Afraid of magical spells and equally amazed by watching them, he stood still.

'Quickly get inside the circle'. Mars's tone made him thrust his legs and he quickly got inside.

'What next?'

'You hold your breath'.

'What—', before he could speak the word, the frozen water under his feet disappeared and they fell under the layer of ice and into cold water. It was so sudden Jim didn't know how to react. Mars though had done it before and knew what to do next. He swam above the layer of ice and was out. Jim however, was still holding his breath and pushing his legs and hands directionless. He then felt a hand grab his right arm and pull him up. He emerged completely wet while Mars let his hand loose and drop him on a road facing Marshal's home. Jim got his breath back; he gulped lungful of night air which was not nearly as cold he was drawing a moment ago. Lying down, he was under the terrifying sensation of the sudden transportation. He looked around, it was the same neighbourhood he had come to two days earlier; then turned to Mars who was drying himself up with his gaze. His eyes went up to the white moon light that was quickly reducing from the circle; he looked at it until it disappeared and only little collection of water on the road was left.

'The sensation does take getting used to for a human. Lucky for us, it was raining here and water had collected right where it was most convenient for us. Look, here we are, before his house. Faster than a car or flight, isn't it?'

Jim had to take a moment or two to absorb what he just witnessed. He looked up at Mars and got up quickly. Looking at him without a drop of water on him, feeling a great shiver from the cold water he fell into, he asked. 'Could you care to dry me too? I will really appreciate it'.

Marshal didn't believe his eyes. He stood motionless outside his home, on the garden; his face eloquent with shock from what he had just seen.

Chapter 9

Tired as he was now, Jim could not sleep. He hadn't slept properly for few days and same was the case with Marshal. He began to wonder why Marshal had been so eager to come to a celebrity's home. The possibility of her being Venus and joining them against the unknown was unlikely. The voice that had been whispering to Jim to unite the planets hadn't whispered to him for a day now and he wasn't doing great in his quest either. Mars wasn't much of a comfort; he seldom spoke. Jim wanted to talk to Kathryn but the network was failing everyone.

They stood in front of her snug big property. The multi-storied building appeared to be a modern structure bought from another celebrity and reconstructed into an exquisite creation not long ago. Jim had met with a great share of fame and glamour many times. He thought that it was all too similar for him, not knowing the wonders he will witness inside. The frontal length of the property was wide but the width ran wider. There was a long driveway running next to plush gardens with beds of roses and lavenders.

The massive steel gate was guarded by two men. Nicely lit lamps greeted them at the gates. The number was less than expected, which made Jim anxious. A mid-aged lady came out to receive him. She appeared to be not really excited to see him. Nevertheless she approached and met them kindly with a bow. Marshal had briefed Jim about her. Her world was filled with glamour and lights and one could find more of it in her vast and wide mansion in Beverly Hills. Jim initially felt multiple sensations—anxiety, excitement and apprehension about their meeting.

They rode through the long driveway in the visitor's car. It seemed to them that their quest life was unveiling a new route here and they were going into the depths of its expanse. The place had a picturesque way; charms of flowery beds and disciplined shrubbery ran along the concrete road; assorted flora and regal street lamps led visitors towards a sequence of colossal statues of deities in two columns to grandly welcome guests. Half way through the spotless road they saw active, dedicated road sweepers machined by cleaners. Marshal also told him how much a spendthrift she was. Maintaining such a lifestyle was dear and by their visit beheld. Jim fancied opulence but not this much. The chauffeur drove slowly, letting them take the tranquil feeling of the sequestered far-reaching grounds. His vision could stretch as far as the point where the large sign of Hollywood was put on a mountain.

The main door was open for them with a lady standing by it. They stepped smartly over the threshold and she closed it after they got in.

Her big pictures hung here and there on the wall. Mounted at the end of the hall was the largest picture of her in the mansion, above a row of decoys serving Venus in what appeared was Demon world.

Marshal's eyes couldn't resist the temptation of a cursory glance on everything inside the stately rooms. Right from the entry point, he cautiously snuffled and got flabbergasted when fragrances met his nostrils.

Their eyes surveyed every fine piece of art but their minds were inclined for her attendance. Mars registered the sound that someone's heels caused from upstairs. He didn't say a word and walked past the door, outside of the room. Jim and Marshal were surprised seeing the abrupt walkaway when the distant clack of heels announced her arrival. 'That could only be one person', said Marshal.

'It's her', Jim said and he turned around. There she was: the planet of beauty; the deity Aphrodite that any man would worship. He watched her from afar, flabbergasted. She was fresh out of her dressing room. Her fragrance travelled to them from that distance before her leaving a very sensuous sensation. Everything elegant about her robbed them temporarily of breath.

'Mars resisted entering. Now I know why', said Marshal.

'This certainly explains why he turned away resolutely with the air like that of a man trying to resist a temptation of getting mesmerised by a gorgeous women', thought Jim. 'He would have lost his composure just because of the way she was standing. Instincts would rule over the limited sensibility he has. Was there a way he could not let Venus enter his mind?' He thought not. Mars was the kind of planet who knew his weaknesses well. He would notice everything about her; every detail. It was his nature to get attracted to her. And she wouldn't mind, after all, Mars and Venus naturally attract each other.

She was a blonde with black brows. Her skin looked soft, and Jim was sure that it was. She was exceptionally elegant, surrounded with all the luxuries of life. As he saw her coming down, more thoughts ran in his mind.

She might appear too girly and a bit arrogant on the surface but she would be soft and kind underneath. I didn't need to touch her and feel her to believe that. She blessed me with a daughter and I want to thank her.

After a few steps, at the door, she turned her bright eyes away to one of the servants who had remained on guard there.

'I would be pleased if things are wrapped up quickly', she said in a condescending tone. It wasn't expected and seemed to rouse them from their amazement.

Unnaturally excited, Jim appeared before her. She looked at him and looked pleasantly surprised, contrary to her former behaviour. 'Jim, what a pleasant surprise'.

*****

Jim had explained everything to her. After that he said, 'Dreadful things are happening. We haven't been able to do anything to stop it. So we got here as swiftly as the magic could get us and our feet would carry us. We seek your help'.

'Quite likely, you need the malefics more than you need the benefics now. Even now, any loss is prevented with Mars by your side; I don't see a benefic with you.

Quickly he told her of Moon's reluctance to join them and the reason she gave them. He also mentioned Jupiter's strange words and direction.

'I wonder what made Moon say that. Why is she pretending to be so vulnerable? And if Jupiter said something like that for Mercury, he is not himself. Maybe the human form has gotten the better of him. He wouldn't be as direct to you about Mercury as...'

'As Mars, I was thinking the same thing'.

'Don't be optimistic to the point of foolishness, making you believe that Mercury's the enemy here. Nobody gets answers in this world this easily. And even if he is the one behind all the chaos, you should feel lucky that he's not hurting you. He knows everything, more than I can tell. I am afraid I won't be helpful to you this time. But there's one who would be of the greatest help beyond compare: Saturn'.

'Okay! Then we must find him at once. I was hoping that you'd know where to find him?'

'Your guess is as good as mine. But I can tell you that he would be in the thick of things, busy doing what is right'. Waiting was unaffordable, they had to seek Saturn but they didn't know where to start. Venus understood this from the looks of their faces. 'Don't believe Jupiter so quickly, I suggest you to meet Mercury first and see it with your own eyes'.

'Look, I know that you don't go well with Jupiter but he's the wisest'.

'Any wise being would never create the tendency in you to judge someone. Meet him first before you try looking for Saturn. Even if you search now, he will delay it for you'.

Jim turned to Marshal, who said, 'She's right. If Saturn doesn't want us to find him now, all efforts would go in vain. You told me he's the planet of delaying; then I guess we be voluntarily late'.

Jim asked right away, 'Any idea about where we can find Mercury?'

Marshal turned to Venus. Both of them were thinking the same thing. They knew who and where Mercury was.

She said, 'If Mercury's really behind all this, then you better be careful. He's the worst planet you can have as an enemy. But he's a benefic. He wouldn't engage in global destruction till his mind has been corrupted. Try looking at a peculiar face or a misfit who got inside the facility and maybe out in the last year. Let me know if you find something; something or someone has twisted his mind, maybe'.

Marshal said, 'He won't let an insect inside the building without his consent'. Jim didn't understand which facility they were talking about but he understood that they knew him.

'Yes, but he might just let a planet enter'.

'Which one?'

'Or maybe which ones. Maybe planets. He'd let his friends enter'.

'Sun, Saturn', Jim said 'and you Venus. You're his friends'.

'Absolutely', she rose and turned. 'You're forgetting one'. They looked at each other.

'Rahu'.

Chapter 10

It had been ten hours after they left Venus's mansion. Jim caught up with his much needed sleep while Marshal continued to attempt calling somebody at the department whole night but the network would just not support. He had to drive ten miles and get back to Jim after he used the emergency line there to get connected with someone at an influential post.

When he came back, he saw Jim just getting up from his slumber. 'There's a facility in the corporate park at Lake Placid. We'll find him there', said Marshal. You have no idea about how many strings I had to pull to get this meeting. An author has no business with an internet giant'.

'I hope you were able to cook a good reason for us to get a few minutes'.

'Good enough to get us ten minutes. He's a think tank. The guy literally made billions in just a year. Nobody knows where he came from and what he's up to. And he's a heck lot more genius than Einstein. He's got all the brainpower and hardware. Not only he exercises power over the internet, he's got his employees who he proudly calls *Mercurians*, in power sector, coal, oil petroleum that too in many developed nations'.

'Only a planet of intelligence could do that in a year. Jupiter was right. If someone is behind all this, it has got to be Mercury'.

'What will you say to him when you meet him?'

'I don't know, but I have a feeling that he wants us to come face to face'.

*****

Upon reaching the feet of the mountain where Jim saw a tunnel, he looked up at the towering height of nature's creation. Beyond this mountain, men had carved out an island where the guarded facility was surrounded by mountain range from all corners. Under the mountain from where they had entered, was a long arched tunnel. They entered it and powerful flood lights shone the entire stretch of the tunnel.

Jim could hear the water flow above them. 'What kind of a tunnel is this?' he asked.

Marshal responded, 'This tunnel is delved into the heart of a mountain. They carved a huge space between the rocks and this tunnel; creating a channel through which a river flows, the water of which is used to generate electricity for the facility. One decent crack in the tunnel and it would get flooded by the sheer mass of water that is over it. But the make is super strong so it won't come down until detonated. This tunnel leads to a bridge that connects with the facility'.

Jim was awe-struck by the epitome of human architecture that would give even the Palm Island of Dubai, a run for its money. Between the mountains and the facility, ran a man-made river which was getting much of its water from a waterfall that fell on the southern side of the area. Jim was fascinated with what billions of dollars and planetary brain could do in a place like Lake Placid.

The walls appeared so strong and natural, it seemed not have been built but carved out of the bones of a mountain. They cleared the long tunnel and Jim realised that they were on a bridge. Suddenly the Sun descended the connecting point of two mountains on the western side and took away much of light. The tall face of the facility ahead darkening in the falling day.

Even as Jim and Marshal gazed in wonderment, lights came on all the lamps and LEDs running across the stretch of the bridge. Illumination spread everywhere. The building glimmered like a spike of silver and pearl. The combination of steel and white stone and the placement of lights were impeccable. The special circular lights at the pinnacle of the building glittered as if a crystal necklace was adorned there. The two noticed a peculiar arrangement. After every hundred meters, flags, the colour of emerald stone broke and fluttered in the evening breeze. It went well with the greenery of the mountain range. As they almost passed the stretch and reached the facility, Jim felt that the quest will lead him to this place again in times to come and that a battle will be fought.

Marshal and Jim rode to the great entrance at the onset of dusk. Still inside the car, they gazed in growing wonder at the building from the base to the pinnacle, more exquisite than what they had ever dreamed of; strong, great and beautiful in all aspects.

The two didn't get down as they saw security personnel approaching the car. He questioned, 'You would be Mr Morgan and Mr Marshal'.

Marshal gave a firm nod. The man was wearing a wireless receiver. A voice spoke and they could hear it properly. 'Let them pass'. The man fell back before the command of the voice and questioned them no further. Already it seemed that the word of their coming had reached before them. Another personnel came over and requested them to take the main door from where they would be escorted. As the two got down the car, it was taken and moved for a suitable parking space.

The emerald-like door rolled back before them. The moment they stepped in and attempted to take a look at the gigantic entrance hall, they were received by a professional executive. 'Good evening Detective Marshal and Mr Morgan, you're right on time. My name is Stuart Carlyle. Please, allow me to take you directly to the boss'. At once they were shown the way, silently, without questioning or much of greeting. Time was given priority inside, it seemed.

Both hurried after Stuart. He led them across the foyer and into a lane of tall buildings. As they walked, Jim glanced around the place; nothing much on the ground level. It lacked half the employees that it could house there. There were cubicles beyond the glass doors, but they were mostly vacant. No footsteps to reach their ears, no voices were heard in the hall they passed nor any person stretching their bodies in the aisle out of weariness. It was too silent.

'Is it a holiday? I can't see many employees here', said Jim.

Marshal said, 'Mercury used machines, artificial brains if you say over humans. I have heard few employees stay inside this place. You come in when you get selected; you go out when you're fired'.

After a few turns, they came to an elevator at the foot of a building ahead where all the other buildings were converging into. Upon reaching the twenty-fifth floor, Stuart showed them to a fair room, light, airy with huge space. It was furnished with all that one could find in a top notch corporate office. Across the hall, was a table, a personal assistant sitting there, as Jim and Marshal thought, two chairs were placed, for anyone who would come. No sofa or couch for comfort.

'It looks like not many people come here', Marshal whispered and Stuart left the two. They went up to the man behind the table and before they said, the man responded, 'Seven minutes, you may take your seats'. It was too direct, they felt. But they took the seats and began waiting for time to pass. Not certain of how long it would take for their permit inside, they began talking in low voices.

'This building has all the intelligence of the world. It houses secrets of the secrets. There are codes of God knows what, formulas, algorithms to get past layers of security of world's governments'.

'So it seems. But even the best hacker in the world would need a map of these security layers, their codes or maybe a blueprint of entire systems of countries to crack them. How does he know all this?'

'He's Mercury, remember!?'

'Ah! Yes. The ruler of intelligence. If we don't stop him now, he will take control of the internet. I got news that many power stations in the northern region were losing their power. Many countries have uploaded their electricity system of internet instructions'.

'I know. Felt that on my flight'.

'Same thing's happening in Russia. Banks and stock markets will crash in the blink of an eye. The world will go dark. I don't think he is planning to pass and control the information on the internet. I think he intends to destroy everything. Yet I don't understand one thing'. He took a slight pause. 'He's here, I mean Mercury's here for a year now. Shouldn't he have done with his objectives in under a day? He's all powerful planet, right? I wonder what's taking him so long!'

Jim lay back in his seat and stared at the ceiling. 'Maybe there's an impediment. He'll find a way around it—Just a matter of time'.

Few minutes had passed when Marshal broke, 'I think we're being watched here'.

'Why do you say that?'

'See those three men across the room'. Marshal turned and looked at them. 'They are looking at us'. The man with a machine gun was saying something to his boss that I could not understand from the distance. He was a man with wide shoulders, grey-bearded bearing no gun. His tight fitted clothes revealed his bulky muscles. His features together with the unfriendly gaze he had at them gave him an intimidating persona. He was the tallest among the three but they had one thing in common—grim faces.

'They're giving me a hint of challenge. I don't like it'. Marshal's detective job developed his inclination toward lip reading. I thought he figured out the exact words this man uttered.

'What's their problem?'

'Security personnel. They have problems with everybody'.

'I don't like them looking at me like that either. It seems like they want us to leave at once. I'll teach them some manners'.

As he got up, the phone at the receiving table rang. The man took the call and responded in affirmative. He said, 'You can go in now. You have nine minutes'.

I said, 'Thank you', and turned to Marshal. Then I said, 'Come on, let's go. This one won't allow us the tenth minute'. As we walked towards the long and empty slim passage, the bald one gave Marshal a weird glare as if challenging to a dual. Marshal let his ego die away to the work at hand. We could hear our footsteps. The corridor had glass walls, ceiling and floor. We saw big mainframes to our left, right and bottom till we got to the door.

The words that God had spoken came back into his mind. First see, observe, and then understand. What your intelligence tells you may not be the truth. What your emotions speak may not be false. With Marshal, he passed the silent gaze of the guards that spoke of impending danger. And then he found himself at the last great emerald door. Mercury sat in a high chamber at the top floor from which he could look down on Earth just as a planet would look down from the sky.

Marshal murmured to Jim. 'He will speak most to you, maybe question you too. He is proud and loves to communicate, perhaps too much. But under the cover of words, he will assess every movement of body, the subtle changes of facial expressions to understand what we want. We must not tell him more than he should know, and we must remain quiet on the matter of God's visit to you. And say nothing about…'

He was about to instruct Jim further when he was cut in. 'Marshal, if he's really the planet of intelligence. He knows it all already'. That didn't go down well for Marshal.

Two knocks to the door, then as Marshal extended his hand to turn the knob for me; it opened with no one on the other side to open it. We stepped in and turned to look. The wide room gleamed with green stone flooring; it was lit by rows of long running LEDs that were installed nicely into the fall ceiling. No wooden stuff, no hangings, no artistic materials were to be seen inside the solemn workplace. Light brown coloured walls gave a decent contrast to the floor.

Suddenly, Jim was reminded of the chamber of planets where he had met Mercury the first time. He anticipated that he would see him in a different human form this time.

At the far end of the room, facing a large glass that spanned the entire side, there was a leather chair, emerald coloured once again like everything else yet simple, and on it sat a man with his focus at his laptop. It was large but slim and centered on his desk. The noise of the fast presses on the keys filled the silence of the room. Gingerly, they paced the long floor towards him, until they stood in front of him. He looked like he was half of Jim's age. With a suit on, Jim and Marshal saw a young man, in his early twenties, skin ivory-like, facial bones covered nicely with fit cheeks and the long straight nose between dark brown eyes gave an attractive appearance. His eyes were glued to the screen; one hand was running over the keys and in the other he had his coffee. There wasn't a fourth person in the large room. Only the cameras at all the four corners added the eye count. Jim had forgotten the warning Jupiter had given him about Mercury because of the charm he had on him after his first meeting on the chamber of planets. Still, he had dreamt of a conversation without a desk between them.

Mercury didn't respond as he gave undivided focus to his work. The two stood across the table and after a minute, he watched them in the reflection of an upturned glass. They slid in the opposite chairs and before either one could initiate, he shot, 'Detective Marshal, you should have cooked a better reason for the meeting'. He paused as he knew they wouldn't be expecting this kind of an opening statement. But that one statement conveyed a lot about what their conversation would be like—unfriendly and perhaps hostile.

Is he really Mercury? When I met him last year in the chamber of the planets, of all, he was the friendliest. Something is really strange about him.

He looked up right after he shut the laptop down.

'Questions coupled with uncertainty of a future which will not be affected by your actions has led you to me. But your fear passed before you and reached me. It wasn't the detective's connections that got you here; it is my will that you are here'. Jim and Marshal had a shuddering feeling about his speaking manner. He looked at Jim, 'How was your flight, Morgan?'

The question unsettled him within a second; gave him an uneasy feeling which could not be expressed as Mercury would not let emotions come on the surface and manifest into expressions. He went on speaking at a great pace, 'Now you can imagine, just a little yet—the extent of my power even in this form. But do not mistake it to be just that much. My reach is all pervasive now to the far extents of the Earth and before you would dare ask me questions, speculate of my intent and bother me with remarks, let me tell you what I am doing here. I am here for humans. I am here for their salvation'. Jim looked in his eyes and he saw his kind—the humans, burning in the flames therein.

'Humans are like a virus. They take host of an area and kill the entire habitat around it. They thrive off their pleasures and when nothing's left to satisfy their want, they migrate. Their quest for fulfilling an unending dream of desire is age-long. It is a meaningless journey on this great Earth, going on and on to some imaginative happy ending. So I am here, to give them a purpose. They must first learn to let go of all the conveniences of life but they won't. They are too attached with it. I knew that you don't get freedom by asking for it, you get it when you snatch it. And I will snatch their freedom of choice because it blinds them; it makes their life purposeless'. His flat face and dark brown eyes showed no sign of feelings. His voice was sullen with displeasure now even though he was coating it with a polite tone and seemed completely relaxed.

Mercury's gaze had Jim and Marshal thinking. Suddenly, into their eyes fell Mercury's living voice and they could literally imagine the utter chaos he began to narrate. 'They will starve for food, water, shelter, electricity. They will kill each other for survival. Humankind will kill itself. It will not have the courage to learn for millions of years and establish itself again the way it is now. The ones left will have nothing but to seek a leader, a life giver. And then, they will come to my feet. I will give the purpose—Eternal servitude'.

There was an obvious sign of anger on Marshal's face; he had a fragile ego that his power and position credited to him. Jim was feeling the chill that was emanating from Mercury's words. He hadn't snapped out properly from the terrible imagination that was inserted in his mind. But he didn't want him to continue speaking and rain terror on him. 'How… how… could you do this? I learnt about you. This cannot be you'.

'You have walked all your life with closed ears and mind asleep and you still don't wake up now. That is so human.

You think learning a little bit of astrology scarcely gives you the wisdom to understand me and what I can do even with a human body'. For the first time since he spoke, he paused just to relish the spreading marks of fear on them. What followed was a heavy silence.

'Humans put faith in machines more than they put on each other. And as the imagined yet ignored danger reaches them, they lose control over their creations just like in your case they lost control of the flight. These machines have the power to gain control over your kind; someone with the required brain muscle can make a machine go against them. Only after it is too late do they realise that their own creation has eventually led them to their demise. The problem with humans is not that they don't expect the worst, the problem is they live with the hope for the best. This defeats them; it makes them become unprepared for the danger that lies ahead. I am here to make them understand something. They will understand that death is a luxury that takes away all pain, the attachments, their debts. But I won't give them a quick death, no, no, no; they haven't done anything to earn it. It is the journey towards it that will kill them slowly. Death is a promise, life is the lie. I will promise them a slow death and take that lie away from them. You have been reading it, feeling it, it is all around you. Your communication systems, transportation, banking, everything will fall as they have let the door of their mind open to fear of losing all. It will enter slowly causing them pain, giving them the feeling of powerlessness over life. They will let hope die. And that's how it will start. The beginning of their end'. And with that said, he turned his heavy chair and gave them his back.

'You're, you're crazy', faltered Marshal. His anger was evident in his voice.

'What can you humans do!?' he said half mockingly, half challengingly, looking keenly at the two from the reflection of their bodies on his coffee mug. Jim stirred and his heart was shrouded with fear.

But Marshal forgot his fear as anger overwhelmed his senses yet knowing his position in Mercury's lair, he developed a restraint that didn't let him do anything reckless. Within seconds, he knew Mercury wasn't in a mood to talk more; he had clearly summarised everything and wanted them to leave. Suddenly, his glance fell on a couple of files lying on the table. *I'll show you what we can do. You can turn your back on us but I will draw your attention, at least for a while and drift you away from your plans.*

Marshal tucked one file under his coat away from the reflection on the coffee mug. 'He's right. Let's get out of here'. Jim couldn't believe Marshal had given up on Mercury this easy. He got up but Jim was still sitting looking at him. 'The best we can do is escape the appalling damage hearing his crap will inflict upon us'.

'But...', Marshal interrupted him and passed a quick wink and a look that grasped his eyes reassuringly. Jim wanted but didn't argue and followed him as they got out. Mercury didn't watch them go. They were not of any interest to him yet.

Jim had his head down, he was seeing his reflection on the shine of his shoes but his mind wasn't there. Just as they reached the waiting room, their way was blocked by the three guards. Marshal stopped and Jim walked right into him. 'Sorry, I didn't...', he was shut looking at the unreasonably angered faces of men. The tallest was looking Marshal dead straight in the eye.

Marshal said, 'Step aside kid', his tone stern.

The man didn't. 'I say what happens here. Don't dare coming again'.

Marshal never had a history of returning a polite talk after hearing the slightest unpleasant tone. 'How long did it take you to shave that massive head of yours? Seriously, I'm curious'.

The man took a step forward. Now just inches away from Marshal, he said, 'I would love to see you take off that badge, will teach you a thing or two'.

'Why don't you also do the same and meet me outside? I'll teach you not to mess with somebody twice your size'.

'We can go now Marshal, there's no need for this', Jim was slightly pulling his arm. The three didn't budge. Marshal's head too was fixed on the larger thing at hand; he didn't look at the men again and with Jim, got down to the threshold where their car was waiting for them.

Chapter 11

A mile away from the foot of the mountain, Jim finally spoke, 'Marshal, stop the car'. He hit the brakes and knowing what Jim would ask him, he revealed the file he stole from Mercury.

'What's this?'

'Not sure what it is; but if it could make it to his table, it is very dear to him'.

Jim's face lightened and a smile flitted across there. 'First a detective and now a thief, come here', he grabbed Marshal into a hug. 'Overlooking us humans will be his misfortune'.

'Easy there man, let's take a look what's inside'. There were papers: classified papers inside. 'How did he get these?'

'Is there something top secret like nuclear codes or something?'

'No but it looks like the government had excavated a precious stone of some sort from a forest in Africa. Here, take a look'. Marshal rolled a picture.

'It is an emerald stone', he said.

'There are lots of emeralds in the world. What's this one doing in a classified file?'

'Did you notice Moon had a pearl on her'.

'Now that you've mentioned, I did find a peculiar light coming out of it. At that time I didn't think it was special'.

'If she is a human now, how come she has the power of bringing clouds and moist in a desert?'

'Don't tell me… Are you thinking what I'm thinking?'

Jim nodded slightly. 'I believe these stones hold some mystical magic and they can scale up a planet's powers'.

'What use would Mercury have of this Emerald then? He's already executing his devastative motives nicely'.

'I don't know but if he wants this, perhaps this is the final element that will complete his objective. This emerald can possibly give him power beyond his limitations'.

'What should we do? We both don't have contacts or power to get this one from the enforced vault it is kept safe in. We can't even dream of stealing it. It's here in this building'. There was a picture of a stronghold, a building that housed the emerald.

'We know the scale of his plan but we still don't know how he'll be using this emerald to achieve it'.

'I don't want to be sitting here doing nothing till we find that out. I know that we need to know what we are up against well ahead of time but…'

'Time… Yes time, that's it'.

'What's what?'

'Come, if I am right, then we may have a chance here'.

'Mercury's too fast and intelligent for us. Perhaps he's found a way to get this stone. We need to slow him down'.

'How do we do that?'

'We cannot but I know someone who would know. Someone who can help us get it before Mercury does'.

'Do you mean to say Saturn? Mercury will know what we will do before we even do it. How do we find Saturn before he gets to us?'

'Haven't you been noticing? These internet glitches happen but are obstructed almost immediately. Saturn's been trying to save us all since the beginning. He wants us to get to him before Mercury's men do'. Marshal's eyes sparked a little. There was hope in them. Jim gave no reaction to the discovery. He was imagining where Saturn was hiding.

'If this emerald is of any use to him, I bet it is to counter Saturn'.

*****

Having reached their temporary stay, Marshal posed a question to Jim. Mars was outside the room, listening. 'He must have left a trail for us if he wants us to find him', said Marshal.

Jim disagreed through head gesture. 'On the contrary if he leaves a trail, Mercury or his men will find him first before we do'.

'I don't think there's anything we can do to outwit the Planet of Intelligence?'

'Sure we can. He's the significator of intelligence. But I have something he doesn't'. Marshal instantly anticipated Jim's answer. 'Imagination'. A cluster of thoughts rose in Marshal's mind; words failed him for a while as he looked at Jim.

Jim quickly took out a page, spanned his pen over it and drew three horoscopes. The resulting figures were titled as 'House Numbers', 'Significator of Houses' and 'Direction of Houses'. Marshal hadn't seen horoscopes so for Jim's explanation to work, he had to start from the basic. He looked in wonder at the strange diagrams of which he had heard many things in his conversations with Jim but understood less.

Jim began his explanation. 'Look at the second chart. The numbers show the houses in a person's horoscope, every house represents a lot of things in life. Saturn is the significator of sixth, eighth, tenth and twelfth house'.

'What's a significator?'

'Ah! We can talk about astrological details some other day. Focus on the numbers of houses—sixth, eighth, tenth and twelfth. You're good with directions'.

'Try me'.

'Now let's turn to the third chart. I am writing the directions which each house represents. My quest began from near New York; we are standing at a place where we are beginning to talk about Saturn. Let's say we are at the first house which is East from New York and in East, Mercury's Corporate Park is situated'. Marshal started using his compass and calculated something in the mind for his understanding. Jim pointed on the box with the number eight. 'If the first is the East, then this one should be?'

'Wait! If first house is east then the opposite to it, which is the seventh should be west. Then I'd say eighth should be close to North West, I mean North of North West according to the estimation that tenth is North'.

'And I told you that Saturn signifies eighth house'.

'Well I'll be damned. This can't be a coincidence'.

'Originally the first zodiac is Aries and goes to Pisces. Now let me mark zodiac signs in the houses'.

Jim wrote the signs on every box with numbers starting with 1 as Aries, 2 as Taurus and so on. Immediately Marshal said, 'So Scorpio is falling in the eighth house now. What does that mean?'

'I haven't learnt astrology in that detail'.

'What're you trying to say with this?'

'The file shows that a facility is located in North of North West to us and the emerald key happens to be secured exactly there'. Marshal nodded. 'My imagination suggests that he's highly close to that vault; in that area a huge network of wireless government operations take place—the place where all data on the Earth gets stored and distributed. That is why they kept the emerald stone there because the place is even more secured than the Pentagon; we just don't see how. Saturn should be there because only then can he cause obstruction to the network through which Mercury causes the internet glitches'.

'You're right. I can't think about any other location. Mercury's eyes are everywhere. Everywhere but…' They both took an elongated moment before Jim added, 'Right under his nose. I mean really under his nose'.

'That's it he's somewhere inside the building of the emerald key where Mercury hasn't been looking with detail'.

'No, no, no', Jim shook head after the third no. 'The entire area and facility has the world's best cameras. Any one tampering with the machines would easily be spotted. Moreover, they only take security officers who have a working experience of over a decade I bet. Saturn just came on Earth last year. They wouldn't allow him inside as an official and even if Saturn was inside the building, he'd not be safe'.

'So eighth house, Scorpio, North of North West, what do they tell you?'

'The Element of Scorpio is Water and eighth house shows things buried underground, from gemstones to coal, petroleum to dead bodies. But under that facility, there's no graveyard or mine. What can be underground that place with lot of water?'

'The Sewer!' Marshal had marked surprise on his face. 'That's it! Saturn's been playing really close to the chest. You're a genius Jim'.

'I had guidance, from a voice I do not know much of. It keeps on whispering to me'. Marshal didn't say anything to this. Maybe it was God who was showing way to him or maybe someone else. But the focus he felt was to be directed towards finding Saturn.

Their discovery made a lot of sense. How was Saturn protecting them all this while and kept hidden from Mercury? The entire grid around the vault where emerald was kept had cables running everywhere. Before the advent of the wireless technology which Mercury was using, these lined networks were very spread out. They connected with every home, every office of the country. Saturn was making use of obsolete grapevine of underground wires to channel his energy and stop Mercury's work of disaster. He had been using these lines to throw his aspect on Mercury and his heinous men without him having the slightest clue.

'The intelligent got outclassed', said Marshal.

'Saturn's the hardest working planet. He mustn't have slept the whole year to be able to do what he's doing'

'I heard that Saturn brings about misery to those who take the road to injustice. Why can't he just stop Mercury from doing what he's doing?'

'Saturn delays Marshal, he doesn't deny. He's the planet of justice, that's true. There a lot behind his actions. We must get to him now'. North of North West from their point to the emerald facility meant covering a distance of three miles. The city had cameras everywhere. They knew that their enemy must be watching them like hungry eagle. This meant that undetected movement on streets was theoretically impossible.

'If we step on the road, the cameras will detect us and Mercury will tell his henchmen to hunt us down. I have a feeling that he has found that we took his file and already knows where we are', said Marshal.

'We will have to wait till rush hour. The system has eyes all over but if we walk in cloaked dresses, with so many pedestrians around us, we'll be able to walk past the cameras', said Jim.

'Leave him to me', entered Mars. 'First I will gain his attention and then once his men come for me, I will give myself to him. You will have a window to make it to the sewage system'.

'No!' Jim pressed. 'It is too risky. You're still a human. A shot to the head and you're dead. We need you till the end of the line'.

'Your arrogance has turned into ignorance. No bullet can stop me and the way I see it, there's no other way'.

'There is one', said Marshal. 'Why don't we lead them to the sewer? Maybe Mars will have an upper hand there in combat'. Both turned to Mars. He didn't say anything. 'If there's the slightest chance to beat them there, I think we should be more than willing to take it. It's definitely better than handing you over to your grave'.

Mars thought for a while. Thinking wasn't his best suit but the tactic sounded effective. He looked at Jim. 'I never thought a planet will need a human's help. I understand now why God chose you'. Even in this gloom, hope had gleamed again for them.

*****

Many roads crossed near the destined alley from where they would enter the line of sewers; just one led to it. In that time of the evening, there was much coming and going of people around the alley. But most of the traffic never entered there, just passed by. The roads were wide and well paved but cameras on all the streets meant Mercury's henchmen had eyes everywhere. If Jim and the others have to slip unnoticed, they had to change faces or make them untraceable by face detecting software. They took a cab first and veiled their faces with large hats and coats that mixed well with the moving crowd. Luckily for them, the streets around that alley were choked with cars then. After their car had stopped at a traffic signal, the three got out of it, paid the driver they had taken and Marshal took the lead.

The three were walking along the verge of the road that ran straight into the alley. Mars sensed someone approaching. 'Don't look south, we're being followed'. They hastened their steps edging their way into the walking crowd on the pavement and immersing well into it. Marshal took an ally which wasn't leading them away from the entrance of the sewers. The henchmen behind them lost track of them amidst the organised movement of so many people. They regained the main street then. Marshal now led them into a wide alley; it ran between tall buildings and was lit with just one street light.

'That's the safest line that will lead us to the center of the gutters under the facility', Marshal told them. They passed the voices of the crowd talking on phone and the tramp of their feet and entered inside gutters. The henchmen seemed to have lost them completely. As they got under, light died down there.

'I hope you lead us to him', Mars said to Marshal.

'I know the place above us very well. Yet finding the point where all wires culminate will take some time'. They walked and turned and walked further. They took many turns. Guessing the place 'right under the nose' narrowed to the tunnel to their right but left uncertainty. It was still a guess. There was no way without a map of the level to predict where Saturn was.

It was cold outside; still inside the sewer it was colder. There wasn't anything in their stomachs to warm them up in there. Dark, dingy, scary was this tunnel. A numb terror had Jim in its wrap as he advanced. His eyes weren't powerful enough to scope the dark of the sewer. Luckily, Marshal had one torch. Hope was leading their way more than the ray of light. For time countless, they had been taking turns and more turns and they felt like they were lost in the maze of the sewer system.

Marshal said, 'We've been here for more than an hour, I can't breathe anymore'.

At this Mars rebuffed, 'Think about Saturn. He's been here for a year now. He's breathing the same thing'. Mars and

Saturn were both malefic in nature. Mars detested calculated delays of Saturn and Saturn detested Mars's straightforward, action-oriented behaviour. Still, even after personal issues, Jim learnt that even an enemy can choose to show respect. He wished that Saturn would do the same for Mars when they find him.

The three of them felt gloomy more than they felt disgusted while treading their way inside the lines of sewer. They kept on walking and guessing the right ways, listening to the voice of gutter water, the whisper of insects and rodents.

'I can see some dark little things moving on the ground. Ah! I cannot stand it', cried Marshal. The two didn't heed him much. Behind these sounds, there was vast waiting silence which gave them the creeps. Marshal longed to shut out this experience the most as quickly as they possibly could. At one juncture they became clueless as to what direction they must choose. And that is when Jim noticed another rat; there was something very peculiar about its movement.

'I say it is this side', said Marshal pointing to his left.

'I say let's go to the other way. If we don't find him there, we come back here and check', spoke Mars. 'Hey! Where're you going?' Jim walked a few steps to the left side first and then turned and advanced further into the opposite direction following the rat.

'It is this way', his voice communicated certainty. It seemed that in the direction where Mars pointed towards, the gloom was growing and gathering very slowly and Jim felt it nearer and darker as it advanced. While in Marshal's direction it felt fainter and distant. 'I can feel him, I can feel his aura. Look at the rat, its movement is way much slower than other rats. It appears that he has been affected by the presence of Saturn. His movement is slowed unnaturally'.

Marshal noticed the rat but it didn't interest him much. 'What aura?' he asked.

'Come forward', Jim asked the two. They followed. 'Do you feel dread, gloom, cold?' Marshal could only feel his hopes going down.

'He's right. I feel it too', said Mars.

They were walking deeper into a long line between patches of light and deep darkness which wasn't much lighted with their only torch. Almost beyond hearing, Jim thought he caught a voice: faint, cold and one that sounded pained. After more than two hours of searching, at the end of current line they walked and finally they found the chamber central to every other. One bald lightbulb dangled on a wire above them and one more on another wire at the far corner of the chamber. The sewer of shadows looked more terrifying that anyone of them had imagined. So far the sewerage system has been cold but only this place was different. It was the hottest and most humid sewer line they came into. The air reeked of sewer smell, flies flying around slowly. Rats and cockroaches were giving company to the figure they saw holding cables in his arms at the far end of the chamber.

Jim's eyes fell on that image. 'Is that him'? A spark of hope came to life. The figure stood steaming with sweat; he held his neck up with eyes closed, there was a clear determination in his stature but his body showed complete signs of weariness. Behind him loomed great number of cables, some suspended, a few taut and some giving away sparks.

Electricity passed through his body but he didn't cry in pain. He was much used to it by now. Jim got reminded of his nightmares where he had seen the same figure, trapped and suffering. 'It is him'. They were sure now.

The sight of him made the back of Marshal's neck prickle unpleasantly. Jim's eyes lingered for a moment on him too and he saw large frown momentarily crease Mars's usually plain forehead.

Colt, one of the three main guards of Mercury, who Jim and Marshal saw at the reception, was standing with two of his men behind them. 'Look at who we got here'.

Everyone turned in surprise.

'We dug a hole and waited for you to make the move. Following you to this rendezvous was easy, considering just how reckless you two have become in his presence'. He had his eyes on Mars then. 'And see who you got us to. The only one standing in our way. He won't stand there any longer'. His sight stretched to Saturn.

'You know who these two are yet you act against them'. It was a ridiculous statement at that time but Jim said it anyway. Surely they had assumed what they were up against and if they were here prepared with the arms, the impression of Jim's words wouldn't work.

'Huh yeah I know who these two are. Just powerless, expendable planets'. Mars got angered at this.

'They're more powerful than you can fathom', said Marshal.

'No, they are not. After our boss's plan succeeds, we will find our salvation. Unfortunately for you, you won't live long enough to see it'.

'I don't think so', said Mars.

'Still arrogant and hopeful. I'm curious, what can you do to stop us from pulling the trigger?' He looked at Saturn now, who stood handcuff with wires. 'What can you do old man?'

There was a lapse of a moment. They heard a voice from behind, 'There's a difference'. Jim, Mars and Marshal turned around. Saturn lifted his head rather with great effort and now he faced Colt. 'Between your boss and us'. Jim had his eyes on both Colt and Saturn. The confidence in the voice that resonated the chamber discomforted the enemy. 'He's got one aspect, we got three'.

Colt reacted and pointed his gun on Saturn. The gun roared; it was louder than Jim's cry: 'No', that he shouted half a second before Colt pulled the trigger. The bullet released in the air and something unimaginable happened. They could see it floating toward Saturn.

'What's happening?' Colt moved. The bullet was flying towards Saturn but had only reached two feet away from the mouth of the gun. Saturn's eyes had turned dark blue. There was a scary glitter in them.

'What are you looking at; shoot them', shouted Colt on his men. All of them started firing but the bullets were slowed from Saturn's gaze; so slowed that it appeared that they were flying with dead speed. Afraid of the unnatural power, Colt tried to move furiously to attack. His men took their knives and followed to assault everyone.

But before they could do anything, they were also slowed. Their movement reduced to nothing.

'Mars', said Jim.

'With pleasure', he answered. It gave Mars all the time he needed to knock them all out cold. Jim looked at Saturn. Even at his weakened state he was powerful to bring a huge difference in their quest. Strength was on their side now.

'Are they dead?' asked Marshal.

'You won't have to worry about them, now let's get him down', answered Mars.

They went up to him. 'We're going to bring you down now. Stay put', said Jim.

'I shouldn't leave contact with these lines', Saturn spoke. There was much strain in his voice and it was only as weak as a whisper.

'We need you with us. We can't fight this battle without you', said Jim.

'Wait and listen', he gathered some energy that was left in him to speak. Jim and the two stood then feet below him and they watched him speak. 'When I sit in a house in anyone's horoscope, it becomes heavy and takes time to give results. My contact with these lines is like my house placement. My contact has slowed Mercury's plans drastically. But his plans have already taken great form. Standing here like this, I can give you seven days. That's how long I can stall him. But if I leave these lines now, time will be against us'.

'Even if you leave, your effects will be here to stay', said Mars and turned to the two. 'Unlike other planets, his effect fades slowly'.

'If I come with you, my impact on these lines will stay but for just two more days'. Jim was unable to gather all the planets. Jupiter and Moon were to join them but later in the fight. And there was no knowledge about Sun yet. They needed Saturn to be convinced.

In a moment, Marshal came up with an idea. 'Mars! Can you infuse these lines with your energy?'

'That need not be asked. I can but what will that do?'

'That should give us more days', said Saturn. 'My delaying power will increase and we will get one additional day'.

'Just a few days is all we get?' questioned Marshal.

'It is better than two days plus we'll have Saturn with us in this', said Jim.

Mars had to climb the wires with his hands and feet to first observe how tightly Saturn was tied to them. He got a few shock along the climb but he could bear it. He then carefully removed the curls till Saturn's hands and legs were untied. All the while Marshal and Jim were pondering how did Saturn manage to stay taut in that position for over a year and how did he even got there all by himself in the first place. Mars grabbed Saturn by his waist and slowly got down the web of wires.

Jim observed him as they were bringing him down. He was tall, swarthy with dark black eyes and he looked old, tired and slender. 'I was wondering, you're in a Human vessel. Your body will need food and water for survival. How did you survive that long there, without leaving the cables?'

Saturn was put on Marshal's shoulder by Mars and then he went up on the cables again to insert his energy in them.

'You're right. My body requires energy from the consumption of food and water. And I delay things, remember!?' he said breathlessly.

Marshal said, 'So?'

'So, I delayed my body's requirement of energy, food and water, and survived this long. But I need rest now, at least for ten hours. I have spent much of my energy and I will be useless in this fight if I do not recuperate. Do you have a shelter away from Mercury's eyes?'

'Your aspect on the thugs slowed them and their bullets. I wonder why didn't your aspect slow their mouths!?' Jim quickly posed the question.

'They have been exposed to the presence of Mercury far too long for me to have an impact on their mouths. Mercury talks, and so did they'.

'I am sorry, I should be asking how you feel now?' asked Jim.

He forced a sarcastic smile. 'Not so well for a guy who has been fried up by electricity for the past one year'. After a long time, he finally had somebody to share his ordeal with. He wasn't going to stop at that. 'Weak body, old age in it, weak chest, fatigued... What else is to be expected from this human form. I can't even move like a young man', he said irritably.

'Still, that body's tough enough to withstand what it did for a year, right', Marshal said.

'Is my depressing gaze not working on you?' he asked, again sarcastically.

'Well apparently it isn't but once it does, I will tell you how awful an odour you're giving us', Marshal replied, trying to add a little sense of humour in the situation.

'Yeah, and you smell like Chanel. That's the young men of today Mars. No respect for planets'. A limited yet satisfying laugh came in that chamber. Saturn was a cold planet but Jim learnt he could play human much more than Mars does.

They left after that, with the henchmen breathing sewer air. It took less time to get back to the street and they were watchful. Avoiding the cameras, ATMs and anything through which Mercury would capture their position, they went back to their hiding place.

Chapter 12

Marshal had found a safe place for Saturn to recuperate. 'He must have alerted all his henchmen. They must be on the lookout', he said to all. Saturn was resting yet he could not relax and wanted to participate in the discussion.

Jim said, 'There's no place safe. Cameras are installed at every signal and he will have his eyes on all roads through them. We have to move out of the city to a place where there aren't any cameras if we want to escape him and come up with a plan'. *Home! I wish I were there. It is away from the city and cameras of the world. But it is just a dream now.*

'He will rule out all the possibilities of our escape from this city. If we are in here then this is exactly where he wants us to be', said Saturn with his eyes closed, lying on the floor; his body showed more signs of pain than his face.

Marshal got up and couldn't contain his angst. 'Darn it! How do we win against a planet? Somebody in the government or military must have noticed all the network, electrical and internet glitches. Why aren't they doing something about it?'

The two could see him move about furiously in the room; he appeared to have wanted to grab something and break it but there was nothing there, just plain space.

'What's an army or a government in front of the most intelligent planet?' said Saturn.

Mars didn't like hearing good for Mercury. 'Thanks for telling us that we're just insects'.

'Oh insects might do what elephants won't. All we need is a little distraction. We'll pummel him when he's off guard', responded Saturn.

'And you think he will not expect that we'll try to come up with a plan? He'll have everything prepared for every step that we can possibly take.' Saturn and Mars began to have the argument now with Mars stealing his gaze away from the three. Jim and Marshal's eyeballs could only move left then right then left again as the two heated up the argument.

'Oh yes he will but we'll get to him before he gets to us first'.

'And how're you planning to do that?'

'I can delay him. If I can look at him directly, I can slow him down. We will have a chance for certain'.

'And he will let you get to him without any problem', Saturn didn't like the sound of Mars's tone which became heavier with every comment.

Marshal interrupted their frustrating talk, 'With both of you with us, things will be faster and less obtrusive'.

Mars pushed his legs and began walking to and fro in the room. 'We must not waste time. What're you all waiting for, come let's go and get him'.

'We will get him but let's not be hasty', said Saturn. They all looked at each other. No doubt they had the same thing in mind.

'You will slow us down', commented Mars.

'Your mindless action will do us no good', responded Saturn.

'Quit it you two', Jim broke in between. 'Sorry to speak to you like this. For anything to work, we have to be together'.

The hall they were in, was spacious with bathrooms attached. It wasn't the best thing available but it worked well. Mars took off his clothes and went for a shower. Seeing the marks, cuts, burns of wars all over Mars's body was a little scary for Marshal and Jim. Those were his takeaway from every battle he fought as a human—signs of glory that would be with him permanently. It seemed to Jim that Mars wasn't the one who likes to make his entrance unseen. He would face the enemy head on and somehow emerge victorious. He was a little envious of his trait yet looking at the resting Saturn, survival made more sense to him.

'Catastrophic failures should have happened all over the world and thank God that even with my limits, I managed to prolong it. To be honest I don't think Mercury's behind this. Surely someone has corrupted his mind and making him do misdeeds', Saturn spoke to Jim. 'I wish to share my perspective on what's been happening and why I believe that Mercury is only a puppet'.

'Why have they made Mercury the puppet?' asked Marshal now. The signs of bafflement evident on his face.

'Since the last two decades, your world has become increasingly dependent on computers. The internet has become *the biggest thing*. The point to note is that Mercury represents communication. So if he attacks something, it will be related to communication. Everything is connected with everything else. Mercury's a genius. Even with his limited powers in a human vessel, he can cripple the entire systems of the world in just a matter of days. First the internet, then electricity grids and then networking systems. The best way to hurt humans is to take freedom away from them. Electricity, Networking and Internet have given you power, money and freedom. He will take all at once', Saturn explained to them his knowledge of what was Mercury's plan.

'In your financial world, they say that one person's suffering has usually been the profit of others but in this case everybody suffers'.

'Then it seems that Mercury was the best target for anyone who wants to destroy our world. Steer him in the wrong direction and entire humanity suffers. But who could be pouring the poison in his mind?' said Marshal.

Mars answered immediately after dashing out from the quickest shower any human had took, 'Only two have the power to do that'.

Saturn added, 'I am thinking the same thing'. Jim and Marshal were looking at both now. 'It must be Rahu and Ketu'. He continued, 'Benefic aspects like that of Venus or Jupiter on Mercury can lead to great inventions. Malefic aspect can steer intelligence on destructive paths. To the extend I know, only Rahu and Ketu have the aspect to do that'.

'We don't know the extent of Rahu's and Ketu's powers. They will have limitation of that of human body but,' pressed Mars.

'But we're not sure if they even have a human body or not', finished Saturn.

'Wait! I don't understand Jim', said Marshal even more bewildered. He turned to Jim, 'You told me that there were only seven planets in that chamber of planets'.

'I did', said Jim.

'There were nine', added Saturn. Their eyes turned to him now. 'Since they're shadowy planets, you could not see them Jim. But they exist'.

'Let's cut to the chase Saturn. Tell them about their powers', Mars interrupted.

'Ketu wants spirituality not destruction and Rahu is always obsessed about something. If people die from the catastrophe, Rahu won't have his ambition achieved. He needs people for that. Ketu too needs people to be spiritual. I don't see how they will benefit from this'.

'Maybe this isn't about benefits', said Jim.

'What're you suggesting?'

'They are natural malefics. They're planets, they don't look for benefits. They do what they're meant to do. They have to be destructive in one way or the other'.

'I must agree with your reasoning. But the way I see things, you are in a disadvantage now', he finally opened his eyes and looked at Jim and Marshal.

'We are at a disadvantage to be precise', said Mars.

The two didn't understand what they meant. Jim rose and spoke, 'What're you saying? I mean we have the two most powerful planets. Mars is physically the strongest, he can get us past Mercury's army of guards. You can slow things down, you can slow them down; that will make our efforts fast'. He was really anxious saying this. Marshal had been quieter than usual. In the prevailing silence of the room, the two were starting to worry.

Mars spoke, 'You're right. We both can do our bits to help you. But we're still malefics. Haven't you been noticing, your actions have become aggressive lately because I've been around you? You've been doing things before you think. That's my aura working on your mind. It hasn't even been a few hours with Saturn around us. We doubt, we are worrying and being fearful of an uncertain outcome of our actions. His presence is instilling all this in your minds. With the two of us around you, you might just lose'.

Saturn spoke next. 'I think Mercury wanted us to be together. He'd know that only you two stand in his way. In case he doesn't stop us, his back-up plan would be to let the two of us be with you. Jim, you must try to understand this using the science of astrology. Wherever Mars and I sit together, we create a war-like situation. Before you make it anywhere near Mercury, one of you is going to do something that will cripple our plan. Maybe the both of you will do that'.

The two had thought this was a team but the planets made them realise that it is a chemical mixture of destruction which would eventually leave them vulnerable, to their own teammates.

'What should we do then?' Marshal finally spoke. 'Should we not get the benefics to join us? We have some time. Can we not try it? Jim told me that Jupiter knows everything. It is time we get the great benefic on our side'.

'But he didn't join us when we went to him', said Mars, now sounding agitated.

'He didn't share much with me', Jim said to Saturn.

'He sees things beyond us. If he didn't share it with you, it is for the best', Saturn advised them.

'Venus felt there was something strange about Jupiter', Jim continued.

'Venus is also wise and so is Jupiter; much more than me. But blind faith on anyone leads humanity to darkness'.

'You're thinking like humans now'. On this, Saturn's right eyebrow rose.

'We are humans now. Only we have some powers'.

*****

'Powers! Jim did you tell them about the file?' Marshal asked turning at Jim.

'Oh yes! It completely slipped from my mind. Do you have the file with you?'

'Luck's not with us this time; I left it in the dashboard. Yet, I remember the location where it is kept'.

'What is kept where?' asked Mars, looking away from them and standing within the earshot of the group.

'When we met Mercury, Marshal was able to steal a very important file from under his nose. In it, we discovered the location of a precious emerald stone that is kept in a heavily guarded vault. I'm not sure but I guessed that that stone could give him great power. Is it true?'

Mars looked at Saturn immediately after Jim mentioned the word *emerald* and met Saturn's eyes on a heavily frowned face. 'Could it be his gemstone?' he asked Saturn just when Jim finished.

'Did you come to know about any other precious stone lately?' Saturn asked the two.

Marshal stepped this time and spoke, 'No we didn't but when we met Moon, we saw a pearl on her. It didn't strike as something important then'.

'My God! Our gemstones too are here on this Earth; I had never imagined to hear about them'. Saturn took a deep breath and paused for a while before he spoke further. 'Jim and Marshal, you must hear carefully. This is most important. There are gemstones related to each one of us;

they signify our powers and for millenniums they have been used by humans to overcome the shortcomings they have and to call for fortune to rain upon them. These were formed here, on Earth; but the most special and the only ones that have enormous power to even shake a mountain, they actually were formed and present on our planet'.

'My red coral should be on Mars, if Moon's pearl and Mercury's emerald are here, then my red coral should also be here'.

'We've plenty of gemstones on our planet, won't they give you power if you wear them?'

'No, don't be foolish', reprimanded Saturn. 'The ones we are talking about have originated on our planets and they only are one piece each. Tell me, you have seen our powers and so Moon's. Is there a difference?'

'There's a world of difference', answered Marshal. Jim was feeling terrible on having asked a childish question, so he stood silent not to be scolded again. 'She controlled clouds and brought them on Earth from the sky'.

'Then it is decided, we must go to the vault and get emerald before Mercury does', Mars said quickly before Saturn could speak.

Jim had a question and now he felt was a good time to ask it. 'If Mercury knows that it is there, why hasn't it tried to get it? I mean he's the most intelligent right! So it should be with him. What's it doing in the vault?'

'You're right', said Marshal. 'Maybe it is just a fake report. Mercury must have wanted us to take it and in case we survive the gutters, it is obvious we would go to retrieve the emerald stone next. Perhaps he kept it as Plan-B to kill us; if his men failed to kill us underground, maybe they would get another opportunity at the vault'.

'Regardless of whether that's the case or not, we must go there', said Mars.

'Now, now don't rush into it', interrupted Saturn. 'He's got a point there; try listening and analyse the situation we could get into for a change'.

'This time you try to understand Saturn', Mars raised his voice loud and it pinched everybody. 'If there's even one percent chance that the stone is there, we have to take it as an absolute certainty that it is there. You're talking about chances, let me also talk about chances then', he began to move arrogantly around the space and began, 'you call him intelligent; well maybe he is above us all and knowing that must have blinded him, made him believe that he won't be needing a stone to help him take his plan forward. There's also a possibility that since you', he looked at Saturn, 'kept him at bay; it took him time to realise that he needs the stone more than he ever thought he would. And let me present you one more possibility'. Now he turned to the two. 'The file that you two talk about, maybe it got to his table right when you reached it. Maybe he doesn't even know, cause if he does, he would direct all his energy, mind, power and resources into getting it. Why hasn't he done it yet? Do you have an answer?'

His perspective was backed up by not only a strong tone but persuasive reasonable cases. They couldn't come up with a response whatsoever. And there fell a grave silence inside, that confused everyone more than it convinced them of one case.

'If you don't have an answer, then I do. The stone is there inside the vault, and we will go there right away before he gets his hand on it. Because if he gets it, then not me, not Saturn and nobody can dare stop him; at least without our gemstones with us'.

He had everybody convinced. Marshal quickly shared the location he remembered of the vault and then everyone started to make a plan to get to it—unnoticed. But since Mercury had eyes everywhere, nobody for an hour could come up with a plan that would make them go invisible from detection. As they talked and couldn't come to any immediate plan of action, Jim became drowsy and paid little attention to Saturn telling him about the possible actions they must undertake. Mars noticed Jim first, then Marshal and finally Saturn. Jim stirred uneasily, trying to stay awake and heed instructions.

'You are not going to your home', said Mars. 'We should be going to that facility where you won't be safe as you are right now'.

'Take it easy on him Mars', stopped Marshal before Mars exploded. It was wise for him to do that instead of Saturn else Mars would feel provoked. Even thought they were together, their natural instincts and reactions have to be dealt with carefully. 'We too have limitations in these bodies. Take a look around you, we're all exhausted. We need a break before we spurt into action'.

At that time, sleep crept over Jim and the others. The last thing that Jim remembered before he fell into deep sleep was a glimpse of his wife and daughter in his veranda—Leia attempting to walk for the first time. He wondered if they were sleeping, looking at the moon of the night from a broken window, not knowing that Kathryn was looking at the same moon from far away with Leia clutched in her arms, watching it and hoping for Jim's well-being.

Chapter 13

The walls of the tower were of great height and robust thickness. It was unconquerable and unbreakable by weapons except of mass destruction that would shatter the very earth on which it stood.

Armed guys went to and fro in the ways around the tower. Jim and the others barely managed to reach the tower undiscovered. Presently, they noticed five guards clad in black. Two of them were standing at the foot of the tower while the other three coming from a sideway towards them, as if going at the striking of the hour to their changes of post and duty. These guards, as Marshal had studied, were soldiers deputed at the will of Governor of the State; ready to act, even kill if required without the urgent command of the Governor to protect the valued emerald.

'Do you notice a pattern?' asked Jim, looking at Mars. He didn't get a response till Mars was certain of his observation.

'There are three guards now. The center one remains stationery looking at the east while the other two walk to and fro covering north and the south side of the entrance. There are two cameras covering the area around the guards. Good thing for us is that they keep moving. One checks to the left the other checks to the right. We must enter straight from their eyes'.

'I can use two of my aspects; one on the guards and one on the cameras. When the center guard is looking away from our point and the other two are walking in the opposite directions with the cameras not covering the east, I will look at them. We will have just under a minute to make haste and enter the place'.

Marshal found something in his observation and spoke, 'In case you didn't notice, the front door is locked. Only men with a passcode can go through that unbreakable glass door'.

'Leave that to me', said Mars. 'Enough heat on the system and it will open. All I need to do is touch it'.

'You can do that?' asked a baffled Jim. At which Mars smirked. 'And what about the alarm system?'

'A fried system cannot trigger an alarm', was the response he got.

They all fell silent, looking anxiously for the guards to come to the position where an opening would be created. They waited for some time. Saturn's eyes were the sharpest as he was up for the task. 'Any moment now', he thought. He saw an opening and then immediately, wide-opened his eyes on the soldiers and cameras. They stopped movement, as it appeared to the eyes but in reality they were moving, just too slow.

'Go, go, go', Mars hastened the others to gallop on the distance.

As compared to the guards, the four were not even scantily equipped with weapons. Only Marshal had his gun. In this hour, wit and application of power was much needed than muscle. They went past the guards, away from their eyes and also from cameras. Mars melted the system with his gaze; the glass door opened just a foot apart. 'Get inside', was the word they got from Mars. Saturn squeezed his body through the space and so did the others quickly.

Upon entrance, they saw one guard right ahead, busy working on his console he seemed. The guard heard some foot movement but was casual as no trespassing had ever happened there. Mars turned after entry and using his hands, he clutched the glass and brought them back together. The maneuver left some noise, unluckily for them and the guard became aware of them. He immediately took out his pistol but Saturn's gaze slowed his movement. Marshal sprang up and lifted his hand on the guard's arm. In the very stroke, the pistol flew up and left his grasp and as it was about to fall, Mars grabbed it before it further created sound and alerted the patrolling guards inside. The guard stepped backward before Marshal as one amazed and was knocked out cold with one slice of hand on the neck. He was dragged to under a table at the center of the lobby.

'What is this Marshal? I've never seen you so swift on attack', said Jim.

'Don't forget, he's with me', said Mars and went ahead.

'And it looks like I am with Saturn', remarked Jim and all the others went ahead. Mars had his eyes on every camera inside. His sight would ignite the systems from the inside and all the cameras coming his way were malfunctioned. After clearing the ground hall, opening another glass door with previous maneuver, Saturn told Mars to slow down. 'You must stay cautious, there could be traps in here'.

'Since when have I been answerable to you?'

'Your attitude has turned reckless more than I had imagined it to be. It is because you use your instincts before rationality'.

'Do not lecture me. We're already behind Mercury and your calculative steps will only delay us further in finishing the task at hand'.

'Task at hand is the only thing you can think of. Your short sightedness can jeopardise our actions'.

'And your talk is not doing that?'

Jim wanted to jump in between them immediately but a threatening thought came to him. He turned to Marshal and talked. 'If the government has secretively hidden the stone in this facility, why are there only a few guards and just a few cameras? How are we standing here like this?'

'Now that you've mentioned it, I think the same. Just a few guards and cameras; this is not top class security for something so precious to be hidden here'.

'Are we in danger?'

Suddenly all the lights went off and a wall from behind and ahead of them came down from the ceiling to lock them all in a small space they were standing in.

'Infrared! Darn it Jim, our body's heat signatures have been traced'.

'It's not the infrared, it is a sound sensor. You two couldn't keep your egos aside and went on babbling', Jim said to Mars and Saturn in a sarcastic tone.

'Don't you dare talk to me like that, human', retorted a furious Mars. 'I've had enough of this slow movement; now I'll burn anyone or anything that comes my way'.

His eyes brightened in the darkness of the confinement and they steered left where he placed his hands against the wall. Fire began to set in the wall so intense, it melted the concrete entirely to the height of a six feet tall man; the three stepped as back as they could instinctively to avoid catching fire. 'Nobody stops me way', said Mars and a way was made out of the confinement within a minute. He then turned to the back wall and began doing the same there.

'What're you doing now?' asked Saturn.

'Making way for our exit; if we entered from here, we might as well exit from the same place'.

They turned to look at the depth of the facility and began to rush somewhat. As they went further, suddenly, a whooshing sound emerged from the entrance. Dark flames burst into life at the center of the empty corridor; armed men appeared as dark shadows within the flames. Seconds later, they jumped down on the marbled floor and started taking positions and more men started appearing in the large flame. It was supernatural for Jim and Marshal but for the other two, it came as a shock. Jim couldn't believe that they were set in a trap and on top of it, an army of Mercury's men were hell bent to kill them; this combined hurt him from the inside, as though an invisible hand had held his intestines and twisted them.

'The dark flame of the parallel Earth', said Saturn, breathless. The sight had stolen power of thinking from him.

'It shouldn't be here', uttered Mars. The reason of its occurrence and the connection with Mercury didn't make the remotest sense to him. Jim saw a disturbed look on Saturn and didn't realise the dangerous access of *Asura* power that Mercury was enjoying but Mars and Saturn were beginning to know now.

Then the four assuming the threat they were under ran deeper into the place toward the vault. An electronic system had been activated inside and from the left wall a net was shot. Saturn thrust forward and slowed it mid-air. 'Get going. Mars take the lead', he shouted.

Just after a few steps the floor under them opened instantly and Marshal almost fell in it. Saturn gazed at him and slowed his fall giving Jim the chance to stretch his hand, grab him by the arm and get him out of the pit. Just then, an explosion on top of them broke the ceiling and the rubble was about to pile them under it. Mars's impulsiveness was transferred to Saturn and his powers were getting revealed with every gaze as he saved them all. He looked up and slowed the fall giving time to others to run past it. He kept looking at it as he was tired; his body wasn't in its best shape and getting out from the range of the rubble took him time.

'There would be traps further ahead. Step back, I'm making a new way for us'. Mars touched the wall to his right and looked at it sharply. He was able to concentrate and melt ten feet of concrete and brick wall and carve a way to the next place. This time, Jim felt that Saturn's calculative action was imparted in Mars.

They advanced after Mars led them a floor down to the basement and were received by numerous guards firing bullets at them from the front side. They took cover against a wall.

'I don't think they want us alive. What do we do now?' asked Marshal. Jim was terrified feeling that more men were coming towards them from the above floor while they were stuck after the back stairs.

'I can take care of them', Mars said while in his cover behind the parallel wall.

'No', Saturn shouted. 'The emerald is more important now. Go and fry the vault; I can sense the effect of the emerald, we'll keep them occupied'. He didn't take a moment and immediately made way through the wall before him. 'Come on, we must go back up. We can do something there with limited men against us'.

'Will he be okay?' asked Jim.

'He hasn't revealed the true strength that lay hidden in him. Even with his limitations, he can do wonders. Come now'.

They went upstairs again and while Saturn slowed the guards, their attacks of gunfire and smoke bombs and the electronic system with its traps, Marshal and Jim dodged and tried to go to the place they assumed was above the vault. Saturn was able to tell them the exact place given the feeling he was deriving from the place. Upon entering a corridor at the end of which an office was located right above the vault, the system made another attack on them. Wood began piling all around them from the holes that were made on the ceiling. The door behind them was locked automatically.

'What is it trying to do now?' asked Jim, terrified. 'Fry us?'

Oil began pouring out of vent on the wood and it was drenching all of the piles.

'Run', shouted Saturn. His pace was slower than the two and he was left a little behind. Falling flames were reaching the wood yet his sight delayed the contact. Marshal kicked the door very hard at the end of the corridor and it burst open. Jim and he entered and looked back. No fire had been set to the fuel as Saturn was making to the door while looking at the igniting vents. A log was rolling down the ceiling. Before Jim could warn him, it fell over Saturn, hitting him straight on the head and left shoulder. His sight was not behind his head; he could stop the log which fell from behind him. The weight of it gave him a hard blow and he fell unconscious a step before the door. His gaze died as his eyes closed and instantly the long corridor was set ablaze. Jim and Marshal pulled him inside right before the fire caught his legs.

They dragged him till the center of the space and realised it was a dead end. There was a way in and just one door out of it; the one through which they came in. And then, gunfire created holes in the concrete of the wall near them and they ducked behind a table.

'We're trapped', Jim could not swallow his thought and shrieked. Marshal took his gun out and returned a couple of rounds at the wall which was taking fire. The company of guards on the other side ceased fire for a moment. It was understood that they were caught. Marshal fired again to ensure they didn't advance. The bullets went through the concrete of the wall. The guards opened fire for a brief moment and ceased again. Dust hung in the air, the sound of the shots had died. There were several holes in the wall and door enough for a see through. The men stood on guard against the room burning with flames. Their appearance fluttered in the shadow of the flames that grew brightly before them.

Marshal tried to peer out of a hole behind which he was hiding. For a while he lay and listened for sounds of foot movement. Then he looked at Jim whose face was covered in fear. The next thought that came to Marshal's mind gave him an uneasy feeling.

'Hey Jim! If anything goes wrong…'

'Yeah I know it is more like impossible getting what we came here for but nothing's going to go wrong Marshal. Don't think like that', spoke Jim with Saturn unconscious on his lap.

'You feel it too. We both don't think we'll make it'.

'That's just Saturn's presence working on your mind. You're not able to see an end'.

Fear coursed through their minds. 'If I don't do something, they will die', Marshal thought. With trembling hands he looked once again at Jim and said, 'We don't have time. The guards will be here any second. You take care. Stay alive'.

Jim hoped that he didn't say that. The clarity in his voice and the conviction in his eyes were conveying that he was going to do something reckless, for Jim. The sight was obscured by the heavy fumes produced by the fire inside the chamber. Marshal, from his position saw dark shapes coming swiftly toward the other henchmen. The enemy which was now visible from the large holes of the wall was getting reinforced. In just another moment, the concrete fell making space for three men emerging side by side. Then having made up his mind he acted swiftly.

'No', Jim's word only shouted in his mind. Marshal went past the threshold of death, he opened fire at them and fire spread between him and Jim. Jim could not see him clearly; he ducked to avoid fire on his face. The noise of gunshots rose ahead of the fumes. Jim couldn't see anything now. 'Marshal', he shouted.

Sitting and taking cover, he felt a lot of heat from behind him. He turned to see that the floor section was being melted in a circular shape. The base was gone and he saw Mars under the floor.

'Jump quickly', ordered Mars. He turned; there was no sign of Marshal's shadow or sound of bullet fire. Forcing the right endeavour in his mind, he lifted unconscious Saturn and passed him to Mars and then jumped.

'Where's Marshal?' asked Mars. Jim was about to say when shots were fired above them and the bullets reached on the melted concrete. Then passing through the empty vault, which Jim realised was actually a set up to trap them, he and Mars ran briskly across the paths carved by him.

'He gave himself up for us; he's gone', Jim could hardly say while running. Mars didn't react and quickly made up his mind to escape the place.

'There's nothing here for us. It's a set up', he responded. He kept making ways inside the walls and got out. Men followed them even outside the facility and it seemed that they weren't going to stop till they kill the trespassers.

Chapter 14

They were running for their car and the bullets were reaching it before they could. Jim looked at the face of the many-bullet-hit car with a longing. Mars opened the door of the rear seat with a great force enough to dissect it from the car. He then set Saturn on the back seat. As a result of shock, Jim sat immobile for a moment at the steering. Moonlight glinted on the windscreen and suddenly he saw the number of pursuers on the rear view mirror. They could not be counted in that swift escape, but they seemed no less than twenty. Suddenly, the sound of bullets tore into the plastic back of the car making him duck instantly and turn on the ignition reflexively. He put his entire weight on his foot and revved the car hard. It drifted at the same spot leaving generating considerable smoke and then shot in the street.

As he was about to take a hard left just hundred meters ahead of the facility, he glanced up at the rear view mirror. In that exact moment, a bullet broke the wind screen through the mirror and made him steer abruptly. The car hit a pole from the left before it could round the corner.

Mars kept his head low and then brought it up again on Saturn. 'Come on Saturn, we need you', he patted his face a few times but that didn't help. He was still passed out. 'Can't this thing drive any faster?' He shouted.

'We're already doing sixty', responded Jim. 'I need a straight route to leave them behind'. Cars that were usually gleaming stood a little dusty in their parked positions throughout. The inhabitants of the vicinity had retreated into the shade of their cool homes and a drowsy silence lay over the road. There was no traffic at all in the streets that ran into another. Jim had to release foot from the accelerator and put a brake on every turn that came after a few hundred meters to escape the bullets. In the middle of the night, they were tearing the silence on the road. He drove past a narrow street lined with houses when he again heard noises of bullets passing near his car.

It was no ordinary man who led the assault on them. It was Walt, the main man of Mercury who had the ego tussle with Marshal. With Marshal captured, Saturn down, over fifty armed men on their tail and Mercury about to raise peril, it appeared that fortune had betrayed Jim for the moment. Survival was slipping from their grasp even as Jim with his collapsing emotions tried his best to maneuver their car away from them. But the impact of Mars on him was strong and his heart firm on protecting the planets; he would not let anyone seize his hope.

Bullets had failed to touch his car in the last thirty seconds. He turned a steep side street. He intended to turn the car to a long road, now less than mile distant, where the speed of his car would outrun death behind him. The car chase on the wide road, as it turned out, became far deadlier.

Two bullets kissed the car on the windscreen and it cracked. The tremor made Jim drift into a line of cars on his left. Just as the car was about to collide, Mars grabbed the steering and maneuver it back on the road.

Jim gasped, 'Oh God!' Mars positioned himself quickly and kicked the windscreen exactly three time at different places for it to detach from the car. It fell off given the speed of the car. The pursuers rode over it and continued their chase.

'Give me the...', as Mars turned to Jim, he saw a rain of burning cars up ahead; all falling from rooftop parking of the high rise buildings around them. Mars took the wheels, maneuvering through the ocean of fire, piercing flames. He swerved to the left first and then immediately to his right avoiding getting crushed from the heavy rain of cars. The action caused the tires to give away a long cry.

'Damn you Mercury', grunted Mars.

The cars chasing at the back swiftly swerved into adjacent streets, vanishing from the rear view mirror.

Walt took out a grenade launcher and aimed at the falling cars. He shot the fuel tanks of the unlit cars in mid-air. They burst into flame as they came toppling down on the road ahead of them. Soon there was more peril of great burning cars on the road. Fire sprang up in many places. Cars kept on falling from top of the buildings and Walt kept on shooting at them; while his men were continuously aiming for Jim's car, missing maximum shots so far. There fell another hail, horrible and ruinous over them but Mars was proving to be in great control over his senses even in this situation. The cars crushed the parked cars on the street, some fell on the lamps, and others put big dent on the road. There were only two cars running through the peril on the road now.

Mars took a sharp turn on the right after many running about two miles or so, they saw the whole road was blocked; ahead with Walt's army of men and behind it was Walt himself in his car.

'Do something Mars', cried Jim.

Mars had enough of this. He wasn't one who would run away from anything, even from this. He was filled with wrath and shouted aloud, 'Enough of this mad running'. He slackened his speed and then, something changed about him. He brought the car at an abrupt halt and looked at Jim. With Mars's aggression penetrating his bones, Jim was getting prepared to face death head on.

'I have never raised a hand on anyone in my life', Jim looked at him with apprehension running in his veins.

'True courage does not come from raising hand on someone; it comes when you raise your hand against injustice'. His eyes glowed red and they looked in Jim's eyes. He subsided into silence and felt a change in his internal energies. 'Fear no gun Jim. Face fear, fight it, and conquer it. I will bring terror in the soul of our enemy. I will show you the extent of my limited true powers in this human body. Witness me'.

'Saturn', cried Jim. But he did not answer. Jim rose and saw the face of Saturn, he lay unconscious. Mars had already gotten down from the car. Jim's blood was coursing through his veins faster than usual. He got down and with

Mars standing at the center of the street. Bravery had grown beyond the measure of all other things Jim had done in his life.

A host of foes were coming at them from everywhere. They were surrounded. 'They must be fifty men and more', said Jim. The number that stood before them could not be guessed. He could only assume it. All were tall, broad and strong. They appeared fierce and wielded guns.

Jim, in Mars's presence had developed aggression and was able to master his fear. He turned his eyes on Mars who stood like he was in control of the outcome of the situation.

A thug rushed towards Mars with a knife on him, trying to slice him in two. A careless swing left him wide open for a fatal attack. Mars ducked evading the knife and kicked right in the nuts. Another appeared right behind him, pouncing over him with a knife of his own. Mars grabbed his face with his left hand before he could reach him; his grasp was so powerful that the man hung on his arm and before he could react, Mars forced his head on the ground. One more down for good.

Two others were running after him from the left when Mars looked at them with reddened eyes; they stooped and anger ran through them so strong, they lost their senses and began to beat each other with their set of weapons. His gaze had set three others coming from the right against each other in rage.

Walt raised his hand for the men to stop going there one by one and in small groups. He heeded Mars no more than a pig in the mud. Overconfident of his victory, he let their guns fall from their hands and they geared themselves up with black sticks.

'You dare defy my master imbeciles', his voice was heavy and loud. It earned Mars's and Jim's attention. See that only the two of you are left. You fight well but you will soon be dead'. At the drop of his hand they sprang forward, all of them together. They quickened their run and shouted to strike fear. Jim thought if they come in singles, Mars would handle them but now the power and mind of Mercury's right arm guided them. He didn't fear death that moment and prepared himself for a fight for life. As he had his eyes on the men rushing towards him, something strange caught his left eye. Steam was coming out of Mars's body. He was turning a little red.

He began to shout as his body was growing in red tone. The steam too was now flowing around his body. Some of the streetlamps were broke, some were bent; some even uprooted. The aura of Mars was too powerful. Men who had dared to run towards him felt the greatest shiver in their intention after witnessing the sight. Their speed slackened but they were still rushing.

His eyes were blood red now and he finally stopped his loud cry and looked at the enemies; and then with his upraised hands, he raised hell on them. Like thunder, he broke upon the first three; quicker than the blink of an eye, stronger than the claws of a lion. A swift stroke he dealt upon the first man, powerful enough to break his neck. Another deadly strike on the face of an oncoming man and he fell like a stone.

Backward he sprang and with red eyes, he inspected the next few men. Their bodies heated up too fast and they shook terribly before they crumpled on the road. Mars stepped over the fallen bodies and walked straight toward the swarm of enemies. He wasn't going to stop now.

On the other side many men directed their attack on Jim. He was changed; his face had a tone of red over it. The first man to attack Jim got a straight right to the jaw. The second guy wasn't lucky either. Jim kicked the first the first one and in haste the second stumbled into Jim's hands, getting his head smacked right between the eyes. Unaware, Mars had infused fighting ability in Jim with his third aspect.

So far, Walt and his men had underestimated them greatly. They didn't know who they were up against. Another attacked Jim; two punches on the face stunned him and then three quick on the body stunned the next. Then a round kick to the face knocked the next out cold. His eyes closed on his way down.

Jim turned around and impeded the next guy who was about to stab Saturn in the car. He ran towards him and stopped his hand carrying the knife, turned his back to the chest and tossed him using his own momentum. The guy fell flat back on the road. That hurt pretty badly; he didn't get up again. All technique and maximum reward there for Jim. A fallen man near him tried getting up but one kick on the face by Jim was enough to fix him on the ground for good. Jim took his knife.

Suddenly another man that ran after Jim stumbled forward. With a bitter cry of pain, his face drove into the ground;

Jim had stabbed the borrowed knife in his knee. Jim quickly took the rod from his hand and swung it on another. This one fell on his knees; shoulders bowed to Jim and got a powerful blow to his head.

Meanwhile, Mars caught hold of a man's arm and swung him hard. He grabbed his head with his large palm and forced his face right into the window of a car. The impact broke the window and caused a great echo. Jim stood panting right after he finished the tenth man, breathing the smoke of the fried lampposts that was carried by the night breeze to him. He looked around furiously to see if any more were left.

Lights glimmered through curtains from many apartments and people came rushing to their windows to check.

Mars had crushed the bones of over twenty now. He grabbed the bodies of a few and dragged them with him on the road towards Walt. Walt, seeing the tide turning against him, pulled out his gun and started shooting at him. Mars raised all the bodies in front of him as a shield; they absorbed all the bullets nicely. And with power incomparable, he tossed all of them at Walt from afar. Gun fell from Walt's hand as he got crushed under the weight of his own men. With much force he rose out of the wreck of bodies on him. Mars stood towering above him and without giving him a moment to react, he caught his neck with one hand and lifted him from the ground. Walt grabbed his hand with his right and immediately Mars clutched it. The grip was bone crushing. His arm shivered in many pieces from the inside. Walt shrieked in pain and fear he never felt in his life.

Mars left his grip before it snapped his neck. Walt was crying in pain but he had difficulty breathing. His cry faded to a shrill into the passing air. He rolled over and dragged his body to the gun that had fallen from his grip. Then struggling up, tottering with his last strength he pulled it up with his only functional hand at Mars's head.

'Die you!'

Mars didn't move. His red eyes now glowing as Walt pulled the trigger. The sound of the shot was loud but the bullet didn't reach Mars. It melted and the liquid remain fell before them. Walt was in a shock. This fight was never in his hand. In desperation he pulled the trigger again but this time the gun began to melt in his hand as Mars sharpened his gaze at it. The searing heat of the liquid metal burnt his hand and melted it.

The few remaining men who had witnessed it were breaking away, running here and there, flinging away their weapons, some falling to the ground. At length, Mars and Jim saw the retreat of wounded and weary men; a few ran wildly as if pursued by Mars. The road lights flickered as if terrified seeing the wrath of a planet in the body of a man. The enemy was dealt with and driven back. Despair was turned to hope and death to victory.

Mars turned towards Jim with blood on him, that was not his own. It was covering his head, blinding him. He cleared it with his hand and saw there Jim, standing in the midst of ten fallen men that he had taken care of by himself; his numbed hands at his sides, one carrying a knife.

At that moment, a scary thought flitted through Jim's mind: *This power is truly frightening. If all of the planets are powerful to this great extent, there's no telling what will happen when Mercury's wrath pours out.*

'It is over', said Jim.

Mars walked to him, his body now losing his original colour and turning normal. 'Only for the moment. Though it seems that his men have been grievously reduced, it is not the case. He commands more men than we can imagine'.

'I didn't think I could...', he was interrupted.

'You saw what I did. But for that I had to pass my limits. Maybe I shouldn't have gone that far. Maybe…' he couldn't complete and he fell on his knees and immediately on the ground.

'Mars, what...', he got down but couldn't rescue him from falling. He touched his body, and immediately his hands pulled back. His clothes were burning and so was his body. He heated it up so much for all that power to come out; sustaining it was not humanly possible and Mars paid the price. Jim couldn't see him breathing.

'Mars', he shouted but got no response. Then from far, Jim caught sight of a point where little lights on top of cars and their howling sirens came hurrying on towards them; winding through the destruction of the long street.

Suddenly, out of the lines of fire that grew in speed and length, emerged Venus. She quickly ran for them. 'We must go', said Venus.

Jim turned, shocked to see her at that place and time. She had a large bottle of water in her hand. Jim's eyes shot up; there was moonlight. He understood what was to be done. In a dash he ran at his car. Venus had Mars with her and she had spilled the water on the road where the reflection of moonlight was seen. Jim had already lifted Saturn over his shoulder and it looked like his weight wouldn't slow him a bit. As he came rushing towards her, he didn't feel the breath of Saturn on him. He felt a crushing realisation. Saturn and Mars were both dead, it seemed to him. He heard Venus say, '*KeidusTrevos*Home' and the circle of light appeared underneath her.

The swarm of cops reached the place and they witnessed over fifty bodies on the ground. They had the area surrounded. But Jim and the three planets were hundreds of miles away from them at that moment.

Chapter 15

Venus had brought them safely into one of her apartments. Jim thought that Marshal, Mars and Saturn were dead. He was grim and under terror. He was beginning to feel that it was an end for them. While he was taking himself to a corner of her apartment, living the image of when the three had fallen, he heard a few whispers from behind him. There was supposed to be one, just one: that of Venus. He turned and to his great amazement, somehow life sprang back in Mars and Saturn. He didn't know if it was Venus's doing or not.

He cursed his destiny; the planets were alive and a human, his best friend wasn't. 'I know no more. It is my entire fault; I should have been there instead of him'. He was feeling shattered after losing Marshal to the guards.

He looked at Saturn who swayed and murmured as one in sleep; his body lying on the floor. But he was now awake, only conserving his energy while Venus tended to his wounds. Mars had gently put himself on a corner chair, under a patch of lamp light. He spoke, 'He had a choice; yet he chose to stay in that position not letting any other have it and suffer the consequence'.

Venus was silent, her attention on Saturn. Mars continued, 'I honour his memory. He was a fine man and very brave. Let's not waste time mourning and think what to do next'.

'Your honouring will not bring him back', Jim got up furious and staggered to Mars and seized the front of his shirt. 'You're planets, life givers and yet you cannot save one good man'.

Venus turned, felt the strain between Jim and Mars. She could visualise a line of spark between their eyes that might suddenly burst into flame. 'You call yourself a friend and believe that he died?' she spoke. 'A real friend will keep hope'.

Jim was stung by the scorn in that cold voice; not understanding whether he be mad or grieved or find the mentioned hope. Mars wanted but didn't lose the self-restraint to catch hold of his wrists and remove his clutching hands. Controlling his outburst, Jim loosened the grip and removed his hands, turning away in despair. But immediately he crumpled, falling on his feet and sobbing with restraints on the floor.

She waited a moment; nobody comforted him. Understanding that only she could be the one, she did not let silence of the room be pierced with his cries any longer and drew near him. 'So', she said looking keenly at Jim's tearstained face. 'How did you escape and he did not?'

He could hardly roll back his tears but he wanted to speak. So he tried managing with a considerable effort and quieted. 'Before I jumped into the vault from the floor above, I saw his shadow in the dancing flames. It took not one bullet, but many. It fell and I imagined that he fell on his knees first and then onto the ground. Nobody could have survived that'.

'Maybe he did and he was made captive'.

'What was the need of making him a captive when he would most certainly die from his wounds?'

Venus looked at Jim in the eye and drew forth the emerald stone and laid it at Jim's hand. 'He is alive. Mercury would trade him for this'.

'What! You had this with you?' Mars's eyes popped out and he got up abruptly.

'I have my ways. I found out lately that inside the facility a mystical object was kept protected. Thinking that it would be my diamond I went there and took it'.

'If only we knew that you had it with you, Marshal would be with us and we would be a step ahead in our quest', cried Jim.

'This is why he stopped all mobile communications. Without communication, no enemy of his would be able to take a step', she said.

Mars stepped up just a little. 'What if he is?' he stirred a little, finding it uneasy to say. Saturn quickly raised his brows and shook to stop Mars from speaking. By a sense other than sight, he told Mars that Venus had great power and wisdom that were veiled; she did not come all the way only to bring Jim this stone.

Jim lifted the stone he had been gazing at. And then he looked at Venus. Her aspect had been on Jim for some time now and he thought how odd it was that he hadn't felt the slightest difference in temperament. His studies had shown Venus's aspect giving a pleasant feeling and desire. The person would gain a strong sense of happiness from achieving those desires if pursued. But no-effect of her eyes was saying something else.

'So this is it, huh! You're seeing me just to give me hope', he had gotten up.

The other two noticed them still looking in each other's eyes, as if reading the other's mind. But it was Jim who first withdrew his gaze. Venus kept hers still at Jim and spoke, 'You would do well with some hope. It is a strong feeling and it can keep you pushing till eternity. And if you desert it, you will wrap an anchor around your feet and drown in loss within a flash of thought. I do not give hope; that is the power of Moon. But we're not talking about my powers now. If Marshal is alive, I hope that you get enough hope to hang on; for him, for all of us'.

'Let us give ourselves a discussion. That is what we must do. This battle and journey has been too hard on us all. We need to share all information and knowledge we have learnt so far so that we know what to do next', spoke Saturn. 'And yes, guesses are welcome so long as they can be turned to actions'.

'We can learn more from your rendezvous with him than your guess Jim. Let's think first and then speak', added Venus.

All of them took their respective spaces at her apartment; mulling over the events which had taken place. Jim never forgot that time in the great office under the piercing eye of Mercury, stabbed by his mocking words and more so by his devastating intention. All the while he was conscious of the planets by his side, watching walls and framing individual plans to stop Mercury. Saturn was checking Mars's rising wrath and impatience.

When the hour was over, Jim stood up, and then leaned on the table as if to emphasize, 'I noted the excitement that was pervasive in his body language. He played cool initially but then as we spoke, he spoke more'.

'He is inside a young vessel. Now he's a young man in his twenties. Young men are hot and…' said Saturn.

'They easily get carried away', completed Venus.

Saturn was up now. He said, 'He is by all accounts very smart, the smartest to be precise. Nobody can outmatch him in intelligence. But he's got a weakness and when the time comes, we'll need to exploit it'.

Mars cut in between, 'You're thinking using your head. He'll have a counter for your counter. Didn't you ask yourself why he is doing it?' They didn't. This was the first time they thought the 'why' and not the 'what they'll do'. Jim looked at him and noticed that his presence had a strange effect on them. It was making them action-oriented. 'Mercury's a natural benefic planet. He would never want to harm anyone'. Mars made an eye-opening point. According to Vedic Astrology, Mars is a malefic planet. In their case things were happening in the exact reverse manner. They were finding Mercury to be the villain and Mars to be a helping hand.

'Is it possible that someone's making him do something he doesn't want to do?' asked Jim.

'Planets cannot be told what to do. They do what they're supposed to do. Mercury's manifestation would naturally increase the level of intelligence, logical reasoning and communication wherever he sat and aspected. The news made it clear that this tech giant had created the largest employment opportunity in American history in one financial year. Which he did. He was still doing that, creating the best communication technologies and increasing intelligence output yet his actions had mysteriously taken another course', told Venus.

'Affliction', Jim said and all looked at him. 'Mercury's been afflicted'.

Venus became a little restless. She said, 'Someone needs to cast an aspect on Mercury in order to afflict him and make him indulge in wrongful deeds. Only pure malefics like Rahu and Ketu can do that; and maybe Mars or Saturn but they are here'. *Could it be that the two are also manifested?*

'Not just an aspect but presence can also do that to an even greater extent', said Saturn.

'But from whom? Are the two, Rahu and Ketu in vessels?' asked Jim.

'Can't say for sure. They work mysteriously; in shadows. And we don't know which one is afflicting him', Venus responded to him.

'Mercury wants to kill us and we have to save him. Great! Just great. This does not get more ironical'.

Mars spoke up this time. 'There's one thing I can do. I can afflict him if I see him. I don't know what he'll do after that but he will definitely become rash and less thoughtful'.

'A lot will hinder us and especially you in our quest at all time to reach him', said Venus. He didn't argue.

Jim wanted to know one thing at this time. It had been bothering him since the time God told him about the manifestation of planets. He looked up at the illuminating chandelier and then back at them. 'I want to understand your purpose here, I mean all of you must have a purpose that is why you're here right?'

'I think none of us know that. We've been asking ourselves about it', Venus replied first. 'What do you say?' She looked at Mars.

'Thinking has never been my strong suit. Yet my instinct tells me that we are here to aid him', he turned to Jim who couldn't believe what he just heard. 'This is your task and I believe we're just here to aid you'.

'Aid? Aid me?' Jim faltered. 'You're the great planets, the ones who run the very existence of life on Earth. What can a human do for you?'

'We used to think the same. But now, living in a human body, we might be meant to learn just that we too need you'.

'You think the same?' Venus looked at Saturn.

He kept his eyes away from all, straight on the wall ahead of him. 'To us, there is no purpose higher in the world as it stands now then to save it from the catastrophe that will be set in motion if we don't stop it', returned Saturn.

'Jupiter has been meditating since his arrival on this plane. He's also trying to find answers', said Jim.

'Meditating in a human body for a planet is futile. What is he doing in times when we need him and where's Moon?' Venus appeared agitated hearing about Jupiter again.

There weren't many answers that came through that discussion. Avoiding arguments, everyone took their respective places again. Jim had great difficulty in thinking straight. His mind was still saddened with Marshal's loss. His dewy eyes were not supporting his vision and his eyelids didn't wipe them or take them back in.

*****

It was beyond time for a dinner by the open window in moonlight. And how would they like it in such a difficult time? From there, they could look out on the starry night over Vegas, only they wouldn't. They were all sitting on a very long dinner table in one of the large balconies that faced the city from fiftieth floor. Venus had taken the head chair and Jim was seated next to her while Mars and Saturn three chairs away from them.

'I had known him for just seven days over a year. I travelled with him, shared moments I wouldn't share with anyone. I have known him as a friend and more, someone who would not think twice before giving up his own life for me. What friend does that in this age? Yet I can only claim to have seen a page or two, and there was so much to read in that book'. There was much pain and guilt in Jim's voice as he uttered, half present on the table, half lost in remembrance.

'I think I should eat someplace else', Saturn got up immediately, realising that his presence was adding to his agony. Mars was getting intolerant to Jim's brooding. He too quit the table and took his food elsewhere.

'Do not despair! You can put much of what little hope is left with you, in us', Venus put her hand over Jim's clenched fist while speaking. 'If he's there, we will save him. But first, you must eat, for there's a long battle and you cannot fight it on empty stomach'.

'We rise on the first light of sun; I will take what morsel my throat will allow to swallow. Tomorrow, we take hell to him'. Venus's gaze went above Jim's shoulder. Mars was looking at the food on the table, and his sight fell upon Jim in haste. A little tilt of head was enough from Venus to tell Mars she'll bring food to him but for now he must leave them alone. She sat beside Jim on the table and waited till Jim came out of his deep thought, turn to her and attempted a smile.

They ate for the most part in silence, a few parts she would ask him about Leia and Kathryn, trying to divert his mind from the thought of Marshal's uncertain death that was tormenting him. And she almost succeeded as he ate.

Afterwards, Saturn and Mars found that Jim had fallen asleep on the table itself. Venus informed that she had to mix his drink with a mild sleeping potion so that he sleeps while they can talk.

They went inside her grand hall. Saturn turned East, Venus to the West while Mars facing the South, not wanting to aspect each other and cause harm. 'Does anyone hope to see Marshal again, alive?' asked Saturn.

'We do not know for sure if he's dead or alive', she said in low voice. 'But I like to believe that he's alive or at least courageous to suffer tormenting pain of the bullet wounds and loss of blood for one more day. If he does, his friends will come for him'.

'We are not his friends Venus', Saturn's heavy voice made him sound rash. 'Having said this, I will do what I must to save him'.

'Please say something reasonable that would explain his chances of survival', asked Mars.

'Faith. One word should be reasonable for us all', answered Venus.

'We must not forget the bigger objective. The world is on the brink of doom'.

'I would like to bring to your thought that we also need rest for we must reach Mercury with the strength to fight'. With that Venus turned. 'Go now, each to your resting room and sleep well. Mars you can take the room to the left and put Jim in the room attached next to you; Saturn, you can take the room next to mine'.

Everyone did as told but Mars had uneasiness. He couldn't sleep.

The moment anyone would enter the threshold of Venus's apartment, their eyes widened. But not this time. Loss and defeat was all everyone thought of upon entering and now dreaming. As he was introspecting before unanswered questions ferment more in him, he began to observe the grand hall. He stood in the gigantic rectangular hall with palatial entry door which was inappropriately big even for that large a property. The hall was so large and impressive that it could house a gathering of 100 people. A bulky hand-knotted carpet of white color spread across the entire hall, a fine addition in the collection of the room. It appeared a century or two old, also imported from Arabic country. He could know its origin as he had a good share of war experience in those countries where craftwork and collectible were passed through generations and generations making them antique and hence valuable.

Venus came out of her room; Mars noticed her enter the hall. She was drawing curtains but it was not easy; they were bulkier, exquisitely designed with an image of tribal women performing their folk dance. Every item placed inside had a story to tell; the ancient whooping clock right at the face of anyone entering was acquired from the British; a wide painting of Lord Shiva that hung on the left wall, it appeared was done decades ago by a renowned artist else it wouldn't make it there. Mars was flabbergasted by the durability of antique items his eyes got sight of. It was mind boggling and their fashion outperformed the magnetism of contemporary crafts work he had seen in America. His eyes guided him through the hall; he walked still in awe and as he felt the aura of the gigantic room, he recollected that Venus represented arts, beauty and luxury. She, in her human form, was a fervent collector of fanciful and dear objects.

He observed objects to his left and to his right; looked up and down as he ascended the hall. There were candle containers made of purest silver; three bronze lamps hanged on the ceiling, they were dispersing dazzling illumination; a black mantle clock on wooden shelf with a predominant wooden case- it was an imitation of onyx. An old globe to the side of clock suggested that she had been an explorer; wanderlust since her time on Earth. Swords, shields, pistols, knives were methodically installed on all walls. The blend of all these threw light on a life she took pleasure in. There was a bookshelf too; behind its glass door; books laid unexploited for a long time, just there to accentuate the overall appeal of the place. One painting had a queen clad in a traditional Indian sari; decked up in the richest jewels.

A long rectangle table carved of oak extended at the ending corner of the hall where Mars had been ruminating. The radiance of her riches touched his attention and after just a few moments a sort of fear made its way into his mind and troubled it of possible burglary.

'Do not worry, I don't plan to live in this form forever', Venus said laughingly, putting her arm about Mars's shoulder and gazing at him. Not accustomed to care and nurturing, he reacted instantly and side shifted. She still continued, 'These objects are of no value to me...' There was a small pause till Mars felt her fingers on his right arm where scars of a battle he fought not long ago were visible. He turned his gaze at her. 'Like these scars won't value to you once we're gone'. He saw at first the look of care on her face; a moment later as a few lines formed on her forehead and he looked more intently, he perceived that beneath the surface, she had fear. The same fear that had been stirring in him and Saturn and perhaps all the other planets—when will they go back to their heavenly forms? Venus read his mind.

'The thought bothers me', said Mars, opening his eyes and they were wide with an old-fear reawakened.

Chapter 16

'Your dying hope grieves them and their strength of the mind is lessened by it', Jim heard God's voice.

He found himself standing silent at the railing of the balcony where he had dinner. *How did I come here?* God waited for him to speak, he was standing behind him. He raised his attention on him by taking his hand. Jim could not find more to say during that moment. He felt small and depressed by the loss of Marshal at his side.

'There is a thought behind your action and behind your thought lies a motive. You can hide that motive from the world but your conscience knows it', said God.

'And if my conscience knows it then that means you know it'.

'Your motive has a direction. That motive in a direction gives rise to a thought. Thoughts have no form, so you cannot hold them or control them. You can hold the action if the direction is wrong, or your heart should be pure for the motive to get a good direction.

'So the thoughts will be pure too'.

'Try knowing the thought behind the action. Look at it from a different perspective, that's very important. You have been looking at the actions so far'. Jim was trying to understand which context he was referring to. 'Why is the question you should be asking? Why is he doing it?' He got the context. It was related to Mercury. The sparkling smile on him gained Jim's curiosity.

'Why do you always keep on smiling?' he asked.

'Because I understand the thoughts. I know if it is driven by a selfish motive or by a selfless one'.

'Why are you helping Mercury?'

'He's my son, just like you are'.

'But you're with me now; not with him. What can Mercury do against me if you're with me?'

'He can do worse than you can imagine if you leave everything on me. I can show you the path; I can be your guide. But if you don't do something, I can't do much for you'.

'What will happen if I don't participate in this quest now? I don't want to lose more people'.

'Such a thought will make the destruction of the Earth certain. If a cow stops giving milk because it does not want to, then what will happen to the ones who thrive on it? If a mother stops participating in her household responsibilities, will the home run? If men stop giving birth to children, soon there will be no men and this planet will once again be ruled by animals. Jim, if you stop, it might mean the end of the world as you know it'.

'Why did you choose me for this? Why the quest of the seven sins and now why this?'

'There was a time in a past unknown to mankind when you in another form of a being helped them. It is only the balance of the universe that has turned the wheel of time in a manner where now, I have come to you. I am not doing anything special in your quest. My work is only to maintain the balance. I come whenever there is a danger over it and to the one who can restore it. Let revenge not be your motive in your quest. They need you more than they can ever believe. You must muster courage to stand up and unite them all. Let faith drive you to make the right choice. If they follow you, they do so of free will. If they wish otherwise, then they will'. The light of the day was coming in the sky, but the sun had yet not risen above the horizon in the east. Sadness was not leaving his face.

God spoke, 'It gives me pain to see you like this. Why don't we have a change of place?!'

The wind became stronger than ever in an instant. Jim began to feel temperature drop. The buildings in front of them were vanishing and Jim saw that he was immediately taken, or teleported to be precise to the greatest architectural wonder of human race. He looked around and saw a great desert and hundreds of feet below him laid a vast city of skyscrapers. He turned back to see the tip of a building and much to his amazement, he realised that they were now on the top deck of BurjKhalifa, the tallest building of the world.

He looked to see at God, who now was sitting on a two-seater. The change of the place and God's appearance stole his mind away from his depressive state.

'Well come on, come along here, sit with me and let me have a good look at you. My goodness; an immediate change of place can change your mood right away. How do you feel?'

'I, ah…'

'I know this is too much for you. Why don't you come and sit with me this time?'

'I think I am good like this'

'I thought so'.

'Maybe I will sit'.

'Well, suit yourself'.

'You knew what I would say and do'.

'Wouldn't be much of a God if I didn't? You have some not-so-obvious questions I felt like answering'.

'If you know everything; the past, present and future, then what is the point of a human having free will? You make me feel like I am just a puppet and I have no choice to make'.

'Well you are part of this system, this creation that you call universe and as long as you live in it you have to abide by its rules. Fortunately for you, there is no such rule as humans being the puppet of God. You are in control of your own life. The planets that you know about are merely influencers. They give you stimulus; you choose either to respond or react. You perform the karma; the universe weaves the destiny for you. I give you life, you choose to live it or throw it away. Your decisions and actions have consequences and rewards. Things haven't been going like the way you wanted them to be, so you choose to say to me that you are a puppet with no choice. I would like to remind you that you're not. I hope that answers your first question and leads to another'.

'If you're here then that means you're also part of the system'.

'Even though I created it, I am not a part of it'.

'I don't understand why the rule is not applicable on you'.

'Do you see any plant influencing me? As the creator I also have a choice—a choice whether to make this system influence me or not'.

'Now we both know what choice you made'.

'Sure we do. But this conversation is not about my choices, is it?'

'Yes it is. I want to know why are you here? Why help me?'

'Everything and everyone is here to do what they are supposed to do. So am I. The universe exists on the law of balance. It seems to be shifting. I am interested in one thing Jim: The restoration of balance and the only way to establish it again in the present and the future is for you and the others to do this together'.

'Is there someone like you, the opposite of you who is orchestrating all this?'

'No, not like me. I am the only one'.

'Then where's the balance? There should be someone as powerful as you are, just not on the good side'.

'The balance exists, not in the way you think. The other half of energy that should be creating the balance is my creation. Try to understand it like this. There's me on the left side and there's my creation on the right. Balance achieved'.

His describing way was childlike and fascinating for Jim. 'But remember, the law of balance applies on my creation, not on me'.

Jim was wondering in amazement.

'Look at that building over there; the breeze that you can feel, the colour you can see. At some point a planet functions to govern them, a planet works to watch over the air, water, fire, land, sunrise, sunset. The ones doing their job are visible to you in the form of planets. You know they are there. Shadowy Rahu and Ketu, they are invisible, you never know if they are there but you hear about them all the time. They have a good role to play in harmonising the balance, that is why they are important for this system and so I had them become planets. But there are others ones; who really create the imbalance'.

'You mean other *Asuras*!' he said. God's smile widened. '*Asuras* distorting the function of *Devtas*! Why?'

'If there are demi-gods like the planets, there has to be anti-planets as well. At the time of creation of this system, it was to be decided who rules this system. There was a battle between *Devtas* and *Asuras. Devtas* won and they began governing the system. The *Asuras* on the other hand had to choose exile or erasure as there was no other plane for them to rule. They chose to be exiled. But for it to happen, a new system was to be created. It was then agreed that they would rule over a parallel Earth that was created specifically for them. Humans existed there also but it didn't take *Asuras* long to convert the parallel Earth into a place of horror, emptiness, loss, dread. The planets were offered a choice. They choose to work here, on the real Earth without hindering the system of the parallel Earth. The *Asuras* choose to work there with the exception of Rahu and Ketu whose presence was needed in this system. But some of them over there can't have enough'.

'Just like planets rule our system, the *Asuras* rule that system. Could it be that *Asura* planet is erased or replaced for non-performance of duties?'

'Happens all the time. Once you're replaced, your powers are taken away from you. Over there one who has been replaced finds it difficult to stay non-influential. Once you taste power, it becomes difficult to let it go. I also gave them a choice. To either remain there or to come back to me, the source'.

'What do they mostly choose?'

'When you hear about aliens, ghosts, or things that are supernatural...'

'It is actually the replaced *Asuras'*.

'Bingo. Now you're beginning to understand. They choose the forbidden, to come here, hide with their followers and disrupt the balance'.

'But they're not real'.

'What is real? Just the things that you see, touch, feel? Your mind tells you they are but only your subconscious knows that the supernatural is more real that you can imagine it to be'.

'What happens to them? I mean the supernatural who are trying to cross over.'

'Anyone causing harm to the harmony of one system gets erased. The *Devtas* do that and the ones who manage to stay hidden, they thrive little on this plane. For them, this little meaningless existence over here is far better than shame over there'.

'I want to know more about their world'.

'This is our world, at the beginning of the twenty first century. And this is their world, as it exists today'. And in an instant, he took him to a desert of a grand city where there was nothing but devastation, broken and dilapidated buildings, black sky, lightning and thunder.

'Throughout history the *Asuras* have been blindly led by a destructive perspective. They believe that humans are meant to be controlled, slaved for their desires. Life was given to the parallel Earth but life it seems had a great sense of irony there. They killed all the men and impregnated the women to conceive more of their own kind—Monsters, ill-formed creatures with supernatural powers. There are no humans left, just many creatures thriving off the much dread that is left in their world'.

'I used to think that only the humans are the disease of this world. We keep on multiplying, spreading and we will kill all resources soon. Then there will be no world left for us'.

'That's where you're mistaken. Humans were never a disease. The population explosion is only the result of the whispers of the *Asuras* that are partially crossing over on this plane. Every time a human creates a destructive thought, every time terrorism is born, it is directed by the ideas that these *Asuras* impregnate mankind with. Population explosion is also a result of their doing. They have greatly polluted man's mind'.

'What benefit will the *Asuras* derive from our blunders? From our uncontrollable population?'

'They know only chaos, hunting and ruling. The more humans here…'

'…The more potential *Asuras* they can create to rule over. But they need to cross over the parallel Earth to reach here. You won't let that happen, right!?'

'Crossing over is forbidden for everyone. Yet those with power can do so. They can adopt creative means to do if they wish so'.

'Then that means only the *Devtas* and the *Asuras* can cross over'.

'No. It is forbidden. If they break rules, there are ways but it comes at a price too high. The powerful ones cannot cross over—The ones you know to be planets here and the ones you don't know to be planets there'.

'The limited powerful *Asuras* and the humans here, they can't cross either?'

'There is a tunnel, a multi-dimensional tunnel that connects your Earth to the parallel Earth. Human body cannot hope to survive the strain that crossing over will put on the mind. Same goes with less powerful *Asuras*'.

'But I can, because I am the chosen one'.

'Not because you're the chosen one, but because you must if there is a need for it. The planets may choose to give you the power'.

'And why would they not give it to someone else?'

'Because everyone else is so hopelessly dependent on living the way they are right now that they are not prepared to take the leap. Ignorance has absorbed them. Indulgence has blinded them, defeated them in their true purpose. This world is a cover that is pulled on their eyes so that a truth can be hidden from them. The truth that they are not alone—that in a parallel world, hungry creatures are eagerly waiting for an opportunity to devour them. And this cover will stay there till they become ready'.

'They can be enlightened about it. They can be prepared. They can walk on the path if you show them'.

'Jim, even if they know the path, how are you so sure they will walk on it'.

'How are you so sure I will walk on it?' God didn't reply. 'I forgot, you're God, you know everything'.

'I will let you in on a little secret. Nobody can tell you whether you will save them or not. You just know it and if you choose to believe in it, then your world might have a future. Do not deny your impulses because it makes you human. Embrace it and you can show the planets that even they are nothing without you just like you are nothing without them'.

'Why are we talking about this? Why not talk about Mercury and his plans for destruction? Is this even relevant?'

'There is something wrong about all this. You don't know it yet but it is there. You have felt it from the time you heard about Mercury from Jupiter. It hasn't driven you mad but it keeps on coming to you. You had that dream about the planets and they felt so real; because they were. You saw something more in that dream which you haven't shared with anyone'.

'Yes, the tunnel that you mentioned, I saw it. There's a river before it and I see someone on a boat, in a deep meditation on the face of it'.

'That part of your dream hasn't manifested'. He took a pause. 'Yet'.

'I don't know which planet is that person?'

'Or which *Asura'*.

'Are you trying to tell me that even if we stop Mercury from destroying Earth, someone else will stay hell bent on it, always?'

'Let me give you a piece of advice. Take one step at a time. What needs to be fixed now must be fixed now. Time will bring to you the next quest'.

'As if this one was not enough, you have planned one more for me'.

'You have to let these thoughts go—fear of the future, disbelief in the present and free your mind from the ideas that I am giving you now'.

'Please, I want to believe that Marshal is alive. Tell me how I can save Marshal and stop Mercury'.

'Marshal believes in you Jim. He did not give himself up only to save a friend; there is much to that decision. He believed in it so blindly that he sacrificed his life to save yours. And nobody, not you or the planets could have convinced him otherwise. You will have a choice at the end of this. On one hand, you will have Marshal's life and on the other, you will have Earth's future. One of the two will die; which one will be up to you'.

'That's not even a choice; how can I choose Marshal over the entire Earth? And why is it on me?'

'I am sorry Jim, I really am. You're a pure soul and I hate giving pure souls the worst news. Don't worry about this choice now. As soon as you wake up, something else will grab your attention. You will not remember any of this crap that we talked about but when the time comes, you will. In order to know what's beyond Mercury, you need to find the one who whispers to you'.

'I thought that was you'.

'I cannot be directly involved in this. I thought you'd figure this out by now. Find her and you might have a choice in the war that's about to come'.

'Her? I don't understand. The voice sounded like that of a man'.

'That is one of the many hidden talents she has. Go now. She needs to be discovered'.

'Go where? What?' Jim felt someone shaking his body. 'Wha…'

'It is time to decide'. God said and a white light appeared everywhere and he vanished. Jim woke up with a start.

*****

Jim was woken up by Venus, who was shaking him. He came out of the deep dream and sat up with a start. There was no light in the room. 'Where are the lights?' he said immediately.

'They were gone fifteen minutes ago', answered Venus.

'What do you mean they were gone? What time is it?'

'It is three in the night. You slept, for an hour and then Mars brought to my notice that destruction has started'.

'Sun may rise but the world may not wake up to it', said Saturn hastening inside the room. 'Whatever happens, happens tonight'.

Mars entered the room then, 'Saturn's impact on the cables have failed. They didn't last long enough and now Mercury has gained controlled of the internet and electrical systems'.

'The lines will only be able to hold him for four more hours at best. We must undo his plans before dawn else this morning's light will only bring darkness into the world'.

Their voices sounded fearful, unlike hopeful it did to Jim two hours ago.

I had promised to Kathryn that I would return. I am not sure if I can fulfill that promise. The feeling was sorrowful; now he turned his mind to the road that lay ahead. As they walked out they had unmoved faces, stern and their mind had the strongest resolute.

'But it is difficult to deceive him and dangerous to try', said Saturn.

'More like giving your life away', added Venus.

'He has long sight, he can perceive many ways in which we will attack him and so our plans will prove to be futile'.

'What is it that you humans fail to perceive?' Venus asked Jim quickly, trying to find a flaw in Mercury's human brain.

'There is one thing that we humans do what he won't be able to fathom?'

'There's nothing he cannot fathom Jim', interjected Saturn.

'Yes there is. We can improvise'. That piqued everybody's interest.

'When you push us humans too far, you make us desperate for survival and in that moment, we improvise'. Everyone fell silent. He continued energised, 'No matter how smart he is, there's another side we haven't been looking at'. Nobody said anything, waiting for Jim to finish. 'He's still in a human body. Surely he knows how I think and what I will do, he knows how you will react', Jim looked at Mars, 'and how you will work indirectly to delay him but not stop him', he pointed at Saturn; 'and that you will use words to change his desire', finally he turned to her. 'What he cannot conjure is a possibility of how we all will do when we are together'.

'I do not know what put that in your head, but it sure is convincing', said Mars.

'The board is set and the pieces are moving. I will not like to give him an opening. The others must unite with us. With Jupiter and Moon in the equation, it will be a check and mate for Mercury. It is our move now, and we will open our full game to him, for we have given him enough chances already', said Saturn.

Chapter 17

Venus used the teleporting spell on everyone in her car. She felt she needed it. They arrived at a place near the facility and now they were just before the mouth of the tunnel that connected to the bridge leading to Mercury's facility.

'So we will meet again', said Jim, looking at the long stretch of the tunnel. 'Not the way you would have imagined Mercury'.

'Don't say anything so soon. This may be our last time, as I do not know if we will see the other end of this tunnel together or not', said Saturn.

'Certain or not, I will go to hope's end with you all if I must', said Mars proudly, just like a soldier.

'Hope often deceives men', said Saturn. 'Don't rely much on it'.

'I choose to rely on you all', Mars looked at the three. 'We are here and I am sure we didn't reach this point to get killed and not bring a difference. I promise you, on the other side of this tunnel and far ahead, we will face the one who has brought a grave danger, that lays upon humanity; it will come to an end'.

Jim could not shrug off the feeling that something was going to go wrong. Deep inside him he knew that Mercury won't make their entry convenient. But his choice was giving his resolve the upper hand over fear; telling him to save his friend and end it all once and for all.

'We both know what's going to happen. Just don't put your foot away from the accelerator', said Mars looking at Venus who was going to drive. She didn't say, only winked at him and set off at a great pace. The convertible supercar gained over sixty miles an hour in under five seconds. With the soft top open, furious wind was blowing in their faces.

Upon entering the tunnel, they heard a loud voice from behind them. Venus looked in the rear view mirror and found the entry closing. The following second the Earth under their car shook, and another noise, louder than the previous one almost shattered the glass of the car. The noise was definitely that of a bomb that Mercury had placed specifically for them around the tunnel. It was supposed to blast huge holes at various spots and flood the place from the inside to kill trespassers. The water made way quickly into the long tunnel with the current over the long construction also rushing and fuming on the foot of the hill.

She steered her car hard and evaded a large stream of water which Saturn didn't slow. She looked sideways and backward; Mars and Saturn were preoccupied evaporating and slowing the streams coming from their sides. Their gaze did just what the doctor ordered but as soon as another opening caught their gaze, water blasted its way in from the previous ones.

'Oh no!', uttered Venus looking at the end of the tunnel getting closed from a concrete wall climbing down from the ceiling. 'The gate's about to lock us in. Saturn stop it', she shouted. But he was too busy slowing the large water wave to have much attention left for anything else.

Jim looked ahead and his eyeballs grew larger. Mars shifted his eyes from the sideways to the front. 'That jerk could have denied us entry at the starting point', said Mars.

'That jerk intends to kill us', was the reply he got from Venus.

He turned back immediately to see that water had completely flooded the back side almost till the ceiling and it was rather approaching them fast. Saturn's power was limited and he could not slow that large mass to a good extent. 'I can't take my eyes off this. Mars you need to make a hole in there', he cried. His eyes wanting to sink and take rest but his resolve didn't let them blink.

By that time the wall had climbed down completely. The flooding water was killing the lights on the tunnel from their back side and only a few were left at distance that was left in front of them. Venus immediately slammed the brakes. Mars quickly jumped and ran for the wall with his eyes turning red. Saturn jumped back on the road and managed only a few steps ahead. He lifted his hands and turned his eyes dark blue to their maximum; the mass was less than fifty feet away from him and was closing in two feet a second. Saturn, even though was looking there to the best of his limited ability, he began feeling his feet being dragged behind him. He was moving back equally with the water flowing ahead.

'Mars', he shouted at the top of his lungs. Mars was at the wall and had melted half the width of the wide slab.

'It's too thick, I need time', he shouted back.

All of them could hear the loud bangs that the stream of water was producing against Saturn's force.

'We don't have time', cried Jim.

Venus decided that she had to do something reckless. She made the tyres roll hard and the car started producing huge amounts of smoke. Saturn was getting covered in it as he was getting dragged towards the car. 'Get on now', she shouted to both Saturn and Mars. Jim grabbed Saturn by the arms and forced him inside the rear seat while Mars turned back and ran towards the car. The wall was almost melted. She left the brake and the car jumped ahead piercing the wind with a great speed. Mars jumped inside the car and she put all her weight on the throttle. 'Duck', she screamed. They immediately got down and she drove right into the four feet thick slab of metal that was just a few inches left. The car slammed right into it but the velocity was enough to break past the slab. The engine ahead of them crushed almost to the half and the air bags opened. The car passed the mouth of the tunnel and then they heard another set of bombs going off. A huge explosion at the center of the bridge blew it into smithereens and the metal fell in the river below. Mars burst the airbags and as Venus got the first sight of the explosion she slammed the brakes. It skidded to a halt.

'No', she whispered. They looked back and the sheer mass of the water blew the wall that closed the tunnel. It tossed into the river below while the water continued rushing into their direction.

Watching the blown bridge ahead of them and a large wave behind them, Jim feared approaching death. They turned back to see the wave just about to throw them into the river; they closed their eyes and ducked when suddenly the wave split into two missing the car and fell into the river from the left and the right sides.

'What just happened!' uttered Mars who's eyes were there to witness the unexpected turn of the tide. They opened their eyes abruptly and the sight shocked them.

'What's happening?' asked Saturn. None of them had an idea. Relief was replaced by marked surprise on their faces. Then the wave took another turn. It started swirling around them and a huge pop of water from the river blew sprayed a wave under their car. It seemed that the water element was being controlled by a strong supernatural force. The gathered huge amount lifted the car up with its sheer force and surfed it across the bridge and over to the other side.

The car safely landed on the road across the bridge. 'What just happened?' asked Venus, not able to take a breath.

Jim pondered, his breath also stuck in him. 'Moon… She helped us', he uttered lifting his sight to the Moon above them.

'I don't see her anywhere', said Saturn. He was still trying to recover from the shock.

'She said she would join us when the time comes', spoke Jim and got out of the car, trying to find her near them.

Everyone got out. 'She's around somewhere... I can feel her', muttered Mars.

'Everyone, we must hurry. She'll be with us if she's around', Venus got their attention back at the huge facility which they then faced.

They knew that the facility was guarded. But as they took their steps towards it, uncountable men sprang up out of the shadows of the now darkened building. They were grim in appearance. It seemed death had got them but they were still walking. Some of them had shapeless faces, others were crushed, many stood as if they died in pain and were revived somehow.

Jim, turning to speak to the others looked half behind. 'There are a thousand men against us. How in the world did he get so many armed men in this place?'

'It is the illusion of Rahu. It follows us', said Venus. 'He should be standing somewhere at one of the glass walls of the building for his aspect to fall on us'. Her sight spanned the entire face of the building but the darkness inside was making it impossible for her to spot any figure standing on the face of any glass wall. A hidden menace passed his gaze over them.

With every step they took, watching the ill-formed men became more unbearable. 'We can't tell who's real and who's not?' said Jim.

Saturn brought everyone close to them. 'His purpose is to weaken us, distract us and keep us busy as long as he can to give Mercury time. Stay close to me, if real bullets come at us, I will slow them down'.

'What about the unreal ones?' asked Jim.

'They should pass through us', answered Venus.

'What?' Jim was shaken with the answer, his eyes still locked at the lines of armed men. Mars looked at him, trying to ignite the courage in him through his aspect.

'Death', heard Jim. He looked around and heard the same word again. 'Did you hear that?' he said. Mars who was ahead of all of them had stopped. Saturn had his eyes at the back. They were now positioned in the shape of a diamond.

Death! Death! All cried in a single voice, loud and terrible and with that they began to move to attack.

'Stay close', said Venus.

The host gathered speed and like a great tide fell on them. Some charged with weapons like axe, knife, machete, crowbar, studded bat and sword. Mars's eyes turned blood red, Saturn's dark blue and Venus's white. They looked sharply at every figure coming and attacking them from all corners. Nothing happened, they seemed to be passing their bodies and vanishing. Venus, Saturn and Mars kept their aspect sharpened on every row of the enemy. They didn't blink as it would mean certain death. The first rank of the enemy struck them with all these weapons and passed them. They were all false creations.

'Any of these can be real. Keep moving, don't stop', shouted Mars looking at his side.

They kept passing down the ranks of the men towards the threshold; real or illusionary they didn't know and kept their eyes wide open. Venus could hear a specific scream running right at her. It was different from the screams made by the other illusions.

Her eyes whiter than ever caught a malformed figure about to jump on her with a machete. 'Stop', she said. It stopped.

As they were seeing illusionary men, they were not aware that the man whom Venus caught through her aspect was the third important man to Mercury, next to Walt and Colt. 'Kill all the guards…', she ordered the figure. 'And then kill yourself'.

The hideous creature that she had ordered turned towards its right first and then immediately started shooting. Bullet fire was easily seen from the machete that he was carrying. It was actually a machine gun. The creature moved to its left, shot few rounds then to its back side.

'Keep moving', screamed Venus. Jim had a gun in his hand and sight to his side so far but now it turned to the only creature that was not attacking them.

'So that's her power', he thought. 'She can manipulate'.

He saw the creature taking bullets and blood gushing out from his body but it kept on firing bullets. Saturn had slowed a few attacks that came in his sight, mostly bullets while Mars melted the metal before it could even reach him. The sounds of the gun ceased for a moment and then one final bullet was fired. Jim saw the creature fall on the ground. After that no sound was heard. But the illusion was still there.

'There's no guard on the outside. It is just the illusion now', said Venus confidently. They relaxed and their eyes became normal again. The armed creatures were attacking them and passing them but that didn't bother them. Jim was still afraid and cautious and he was proceeding within an inch of Mars.

They came to the last line of them where Mars looked up for cameras, took the gun from Jim, raised his hand and pulled the trigger. Three rounds he fired exactly at the targets. 'If you want to have eyes on us, you will have to face us', he shouted. It was directed to the creator of the illusion. The creatures vanished right after the last camera was shot. Over the area, rang his clear voice. He tossed the gun back at Jim.

They entered and as they were passing the initial level, many sad faces of working women and men looked out at them from their cubicles. Jim halted.

Saturn noticed. 'Don't stop Jim, they are unreal, all of them. He's playing with your mind. Don't…' His sight fell on dead bodies, swinging on chains in the air. He removed his eyes from them and placed his attention of Venus who was taking the lead now.

For long they walked till the cold long corridor. They were extra cautious. Mars and Saturn specifically were rolling their eye balls everywhere to stay protected. Suddenly, a few deformed monsters shaped in the likeness of half ravening wolf and half bear made a scary grunt and ran towards them from across the hall. From the back side, great beasts, twenty feet tall, stamping the floor went for the kill. Jim's mental resistance to the fearsome illusion was now stout. The illusion intensified inside. The floor began to melt and the bottom blazed into the mouth of a volcano. Lava was simmering underneath and was about to blast on them. But that didn't stop them.

Finally when nothing could stop them from advancing, everything became normal. The illusion vanished.

'No aspect falls on us now?' as Jim said it, there was utter quiet around them.

'It seems that darkness is passing', said Venus, 'but don't be mistaken. It still lies heavy everywhere'.

Inside, there was limited light. It seemed that it was there for a purpose to make only repulsive and frightening sights visible. Right ahead of them, a hideous shape appeared from the shadows, very tall, hooded and cloaked in black. The face wasn't covered but there was no face there; only complete darkness inside. He halted before Jim, who tried avoiding him.

His finger slowly rose to Jim's chest. There was no skin on it; pure skeleton. 'You are a coward who left your only friend to die'. Jim's movement slackened. The illusion was aiming to hurt him on his weak spot. 'See what you have done to your friend'. He didn't heed him much but immediately clouds gathered all over them; dark clouds. Thunder ran in them and flashes of searing lightening rose.

'Jim, help me Jim', the voice was awfully similar to Marshal's. Jim looked ahead and got a jolt that shook him till his knees. The voice was coming from a shadow that loomed in the next level ahead of them. In another moment, Marshal appeared from it, dragging his blood covered body; his legs dissected from it. 'Help me Jim, save me'. Horror fell on him instantly. Jim's hands drooped on his sides. All halted. For a moment, they were still.

'It is not real, Jim. I can tell you that', said Mars. 'His eyes turned red at the body but there was no effect on it'.

'Why did you leave me Jim? Why did you let them kill me?' the image of Marshal said as it crawled further.

'Close your eyes. It's not him', Mars raised his tone.

'I will not forgive you Jim. You have done me wrong', he cried in immense pain. His eyes were tear filled and the drops had reached till the end of his jaw.

'No, no, no', Jim shouted to the top of his lungs and began firing all the rounds on the hideous shape first. Bullets passed its body and it vanished in air. Then Jim raised his aim to the floors above and shot in every direction. 'Stop it, I'll kill you for this', he shouted every time he pulled the trigger with force. Fragments of stone, steel and glasses fell on the ground as he kept on shooting aimlessly till he emptied his gun.

A great black shape, foul and threatening in one of the topmost floors loomed up against Jim's futile rage. It stood there still, silent, watching Jim before it went back into the darkness from where it emerged. Jim's chest had been rising and falling rapidly and the color of his face had grown red. He saw it watching him with deadly gleam of eyes and before the others could see it, he turned and said, 'Let's go and put an end to this'.

Marshal's illusion was gone. They passed the area and ran on a windless path. Light was dimming onto an open space where there were just pillars, and open air now. No roof on top of them, no escalator, no elevator, no floors. The columns were running tall to the far reach of the black sky from where no end could be seen. Suddenly the silence was broken and they heard behind them cries of a demon-like creature. Such sound was not heard in the hallowed places of the facility before and it felt more real than anything else.

'There must be an elevator around here somewhere', said Saturn quickly. He tried to avoid the scream that seemed familiar to him. It was a scream that had almost awakened a buried fear.

Jim remembered the exact position of where he last entered the elevator from. He went ahead of them and stretched his hand. 'It should be…', he touched something which their eyes could only see as thin air. 'Here', he said. The inside of the elevator appeared before them as the door opened for them. They sprang forward to the inside and Jim pressed for the topmost floor.

'What was that?' asked Jim.

'It was the feeling of a foul and very powerful creature; part dragon part gargoyle with dark flames. This world must not see Kalil again. I do not know why Rahu gave us the illusion of the most dreaded creature. What does he intend to conjure?' Venus was as shaken as the other two as she spoke. But they didn't show this to him.

'Why didn't he just destroy this way up?' asked Mars.

'Because that overconfident fool didn't expect us to reach here', answered Saturn. 'Don't worry Venus. Kalil will never set a foot on this plane. Rahu can only make futile attempts to scare us'.

'What if they cut the line when we are at a floor high from the ground?' asked Mars.

'Then I'll slow our fall and give you time to make way out of it. Come on in', Saturn answered. Mars quickly entered and Jim pressed the switch for the topmost floor. All of them saw a fire in Jim's eyes and how the determination to save his friend, who they were not certain was alive, enabled him to thrust down his dread.

At last, they came to the face of the chamber before Mercury's lair; they found no guard there. It seemed that the facility was either vacated or every armed person was killed downstairs. Venus had an uncomfortable feeling that most of what they had done was somehow foreseen by Mercury and shared with Rahu. She also felt that much was guessed of what they could do together.

'His main men have been dealt with. Now it is just him and the pure malefics that we will find next', said Mars. They moved ahead and suddenly a voice fell on them. 'You do not understand the mystery of misery when you see it. I am the manifestation of your defeat'. They halted.

'You are a coward Rahu; hiding and giving life to your heinous thoughts by corrupting others', Saturn was goaded to respond even though it wasn't in his nature but Mars's presence was impacting him.

They hastened along the path to the emerald door. It stood wide open and Mercury sat at his seat working his eyes and fingers on his system. He was possessed; under the aspect of a malefic. It was easily seen by the sweat that he was covered in and by his exhausted look.

Mars always had enmity with him. He didn't like that they were not paid attention towards and in angst, he looked at the large lights up the ceiling but they didn't sparkle heavily and came down burning. That was odd for him to witness. In the rays of weak light, a long pointed shadow entered the hall from the left wall. The entire chamber was an illusion and they realised it as the walls were fading slowly. There was a breeze that they felt and it was heavy and cold. In the fraction of a moment, everything around them vanished and they only saw the chair, the table and Mercury in front of them. The ceiling was gone and what presented was the open starry sky with the moon on top of them. They were at the roof of the building and there was no railing at the ends of the space. Darkness had already been felt by everyone inside, and this time they would see its personification. It was time Rahu stood before all of them, out of his hiding.

Nobody spoke for a brief moment. Jim was feeling an overwhelming dark aura around him. Mars tore the silence,

'This is your work *Asura*; *Devtas* at war with *Devtas.* I had sensed it from the beginning. Only you can love such a foul deed'.

There was a loud laughter that came from the darkness inside the face of the figure. It was similar to the one they saw at the last level—cloaked but with a dark face inside. The eyebrows were thick, black eyes, lips thick as well with prolonged teeth making him seem like a demon. It was irksome for everyone. He began to move around Mercury while speaking, 'Friendship is so easily divided through the manipulation of mind. This was my doing. How could I escape the temptation of seeing my work in motion like this? Yet I waited too long, hidden from your eyes till the edge of the last moment where you and the others lie helpless before me'. He looked at Jim infusing a slight fear in him. Jim backed a little.

'And the great Jim Morgan, the one who God believed would unite the planets despite their differences. I feel the most pity for you. I dislike the thought of laying my finger on the sore you feel; oh wait! I love the thought of it', and then came another round of laughter from inside the hood. 'Marshal died because of you and your family will also die because of you, you insect'.

'Marshal's alive. We know you want the emerald stone', Jim took it out from his pocket and held it before Rahu. 'Tell me where he is'.

'So naïve, so gullible, so blind', he responded and turned to Mercury. 'None of you are aware in the slightest what I really want'. He turned to face them now, standing right next to strained Mercury. 'Yes, Marshal is alive but his life hangs by a thread. I let him live till now because I wanted you to see and learn that no matter what you do, in the end you will lose everything'. His left hand stretched outright and gestured across the table. Underneath it, Marshal appeared. His body terrible wounded; he had lost a lot of blood and the stains were covering his clothes.

'Marshal!', Jim uttered. 'Marshal…'

'Stay where you are human'. Rahu said, 'Your focus shifted to Mercury, as I had planned. He did a great job as a genius that he is but then I came here. I made his men listen to my words of corruption. Beautiful, isn't it? A few words can steer you so easily. I had them dedicated to my work and all the while they were thinking that they're really doing Mercury's job'.

'He's buying Mercury time, stop him before he—', Mercury's loud scream of pain interrupted Venus. He shrieked and shrieked more. Torment was evident in his tone and then he went back to normal.

All of them looked at him and couldn't understand the plight he was in.

'My target has always been you Jim. With Mars's influence, you talked yourself into believing that you were the chosen one. You created a self-fulfilling prophecy. You thought uniting the planets would help you finish this quest. You had it all wrong. You don't even know who your true enemy is and what you're up against'.

'Where is Ketu?' shouted Saturn. 'Without him, you cannot pollute Mercury's brain'. Rahu turned away from them and their eyes fell on Mercury again.

'Answer *Asura*! Where is Ketu?' shouted Mars. The next moment, the arms of the large emerald chair came to life. It was as if they were green hands. The right one first lengthened itself and wound its way around Mercury then it was the left one that interlinked the first and made a tight chain. They bound him. The top of the hands covered Mercury's ears and head.

'Oh no! It can't be', said Saturn, completely shocked.

'You should have known better Saturn. We two are shadows and we cannot take a human form, at least for now. While your attention did turn to me, Ketu had the most important role to play in this. We could not let Mercury gain even the fraction of a second and think a way out of my plan. So Ketu remained a throne, separating Mercury's intelligence from his path. Nobody could develop suspicion on a chair'. Ketu was shaped now to look tight and awkward with his throne body wrapped around Mercury. The glowing green emerald chair now turned dirty and the sight was unsettling for the rest.

Jim was shocked the most. 'Why didn't I think about it earlier? Rahu has an obsessive nature. Ketu doesn't care about materialistic things. But he's part of Rahu—the body part. Rahu amplifies while Ketu absorbs and doesn't reflect. Rahu went on amplifying Mercury's desire to interconnect every network while Ketu detached him from the purpose of a safe world and drifted him into destroying it', he thought.

Jim thought it was time they be stopped. He looked at Mars first. 'Even though he is hard and straightforward, he should show sound judgment in this situation. Maybe his aspect will hit the two of them hard', he thought. Then he looked at Saturn. 'He is less reckless than Mars and has a strong resolute but in the need of the hour, I need someone who could overwhelm both Ketu and Rahu. Moon should be here by now. Maybe her power over the waves can do something. If she can strike the place with towering waves of water, maybe we can destroy this facility and save the Earth. But that might kill everyone here. We must take a chance and stall Rahu till she arrives. Time's running short; she must arrive quickly'.

'Your aspects won't work on us', said Rahu and drew Jim's eyes. 'Don't look shocked. You're forgetting. They're humans now and their aspects can only work on objects or living beings. We're neither. We're shadows. I never wanted the world to be destroyed. If I destroy it, what will I rule and conquer?! This world is mine and everyone will be my slave in it'.

Mars quickly spoke, 'You are but a shadow and only two. Our number and power outmatches you. Our aspects are supernatural and they will hurt you too. Soon we will cripple your heinous motive and before your eyes, you will see your demise'.

'You are right. Your number is far greater than mine alone and Ketu is busy with Mercury. So I knew it would come to this. That is why I will make you fight your own'.

'There is no planet around us. We will not allow you to spread your affliction to anyone', said Venus.

'Again, the company of these two makes you less sighted. She's here and I will make her conjure death for you all'.

They sensed the presence of a planet. Down below, Moon had placed her first step after the bridge and she was advancing slowly. In her presence, the Moon up in the sky was shining brighter on them. Moon's coming was like the incoming of a white light into a dark place and she came with her usual calm. But the wind at the top was howling more than ever now. A storm was growing. In an instant, there seemed endless whispers of words in a language Jim had not heard before. But the planets understood it. Rahu's voice was reaching Moon's ears and making her see something horrible: The view of her special children getting slaughtered and killed.

'He's trying to afflict Moon. She's the target', said Venus. Fear grew on their minds as they could not stop his voice that spread across the facility. 'Saturn quickly, stop him'. Saturn gazed sharply at Rahu and it slowed the flutter of cloak in sharp winds drastically. But the voice was still there at its usual pace'.

'It is my voice and those are my words which you hear. You cannot stop me because I am not doing that. My pawn is', said Rahu.

Mars understood in an instant. Rahu was distracting them through meaningless words. There was a system at the facility which magnified Rahu's illusion. It was Mercury who, still under a spell, was sending that illusion from Ketu's body, the throne, to Moon down at the ground. He looked at Ketu to burn it but suddenly, the throne and Mercury disappeared. Saturn had slowed Rahu and so his illusion of the two also disappeared'.

'Where are they?' Jim was shocked just like the others. They appeared at the far end of the roof with Marshal on the ground. The sight of the planets could not reach them for the aspect to work.

'Stop it Rahu! There's no telling what will happen if Moon's rage is unleash. Do not play with fire or you will be burnt', said Mars.

'I intend to do as I am doing now and it is not I who will get burnt. It is you'. Jim's eyes widened on the realisation that he had been a pawn in Rahu's hand from the beginning. 'Only you and your friend could assemble the planets which is what I wanted. Now watch before you as one friend kills the rest'.

And then his voice stopped. There was utter silence, more dreadful than those whispers. They all felt it like it was the calm before the storm. A chill breeze started pouring inside the chambers, everything started shaking. Then a blast of an unprecedented noise shattered the glassed of the facility.

'Oh no', said Saturn, looking around. A groping horror seized him. And then the storm ceased momentarily before they saw huge waves of water climbing higher and higher from the river below.

And as Jim watched, it seemed to him that her control was overthrown by remorse. The feeling of watching her special children die had snapped in her motherly nourishment. There were tears in that once tearless and calm face. Moon was outraged and her eyes were like blue blood that humans had never seen. It became more unbearable than the wrath of Mars. Their knees shook and they trembled.

The building trembled. Watching Moon's wrath, their blood ran chill.

The stream of water was flowing upwards reaching high, standing knife-edged against the sky far above the building, surrounding it. It covered the rays of the Moon in the sky and closed shadow on the facility.

'Tell me this is another one of Rahu's illusions', asked Jim, biting his tongue.

'No, this one is real'. Wherever Moon came, hearts would lift but now she was the reason of it sinking.

The hundreds of feet tall water waves now had the facility surrounded entirely. All of them watched it cover them from all sides. Rahu and Ketu slowly disappeared into shadows as the planets didn't have sight on them. Mercury was finally set free and his body fell next to Marshal's.

'I will banish you to the parallel Earth Rahu for hurting my children', Moon's cry was not heard by anyone but only herself. She stretched her hand and clutched it. The waves began to hit the building from many sides like long tentacles of a sea-monster. The left of the facility took the first hit and metal crushed into metal from the impact. The other tentacles started hitting the building and crushing the concrete, glass and metal.

'Jim, Mars, go and protect Marshal and Mercury', screamed Saturn. 'Venus, stay with me. I don't know if I can stop a tentacle. You must manipulate me and force me to put all I got into my gaze'. Mars and Jim had already made a run for the corner where their friends lay. Saturn and Venus too ran behind them.

A huge tentacle swirled around Mars and Jim and stopped to strike. Mars looked at it from his reddened eyes. Some of the water boiled into vapours while the rest hit the floor just inches away from their feet. The floor fell down into the floors below but they were able to jump and avoid the fall. 'Stay with me Jim. The tentacle is too strong. I can just boil a little section of it', said Mars and they rushed near Mercury and Marshal.

Cracks were running all around the walls of the building as the tentacles relentlessly struck them. Water had already filled every corner of the building and it was most certainly going to break in a matter of a minute.

A tentacle attacked Saturn and Venus. He was able to slow it but not much. 'I can't hold it much longer, she's too powerful'.

'Saturn run as fast as you can with me before it reaches us and keeps your eyes open to the max'.

They were barely able to miss the hit and avoid getting crushed under its mass. While Mars was also barely managing to stop the tentacles that were aimed to kill them, Jim reached the fallen friends. In a few moments, the other two also reached the four.

'What do we do now? She's too powerful. Even my manipulation can't make Saturn slow much of the tentacles', cried Venus.

'She won't stop till this facility is destroyed', said Mars.

Jim looked around and saw the table there and then his eyes went up to Saturn who was already exhausted slowing the mass of tentacles.

'Everyone, quickly get on the table. Mars, drag us and kick the table off the roof. Saturn, we need you for this', he told everyone. Mars looked at the table and then at Saturn and realised what Jim was upto.

'Everyone quickly', he shouted. Jim took Marshal in his arms while Venus got Mercury and they sat on the table.

'Grab the table tightly, don't let your hand go off it', screamed Jim. Venus nodded. Their one hand on their partner and the other clutched the table from the side. 'Now, Mars', he shouted.

'Saturn', screamed Mars. Mars was dragging the table with his might and Saturn turned towards it. The tentacle that was slowed now had no gaze over it. It increased in volume and dimension and rose higher and higher for a final blow on the building and so did the other tentacles.

'Grab tight', said Venus. Saturn jumped on the table and as he did Mars dragged it down the roof and jumped on it. All of them fell from the top of the building and before they met the ground, Jim signed for the delaying aspect, 'Saturn'.

Saturn gazed at the table and all of them. Before they developed contact with the ground, it slowed its fall mid-air and the table along with everyone over it appeared floating in the air just inches away from the ground.

'Quickly, get down and away from the table', Saturn restricted his gaze on the table and everyone was freed from his side. They felt a jerk first on the hands as the gaze was released but they were able to balance. They got off the table and safely landed on the ground and ran away from it. Mars had the two over his shoulders. Saturn quickly got off after them and ran away from the table with his sight at it. As he made a safe distance, he blinked and the power of the gaze vanished making the table fall on the ground with brutal force and it broke and spilt with fragments jumping everywhere.

They stopped and took a momentary breath of relief. 'Good call', said Mars to Jim. He nodded in response.

'The threat still lingers all around you', Rahu whispered from their back side. They turned rather abruptly.

'How in the world are you still here?' thought Jim.

'Look around you', the waves were strongest at that moment and the tentacles, it seemed would hit the building for the last time and all of it would fall over them, thereby killing them. 'I am here just to see you all die'. They stood, in terror—Their aspects not working on Rahu.

It was six in the morning. The sun reached its height across the horizon and the first light of the day was about to enter the atmosphere. Suddenly Jim remembered the words of Jupiter. *When all options are lost but one, you will have to make a choice between a Benefic and a Malefic.*

'Sun is a mild malefic, he is also a mild benefic. I don't have to choose a benefic or malefic, I have to choose the light of the Sun', Jim thought and a blessing rained over him.

Jim looked up and the Sun, which was hidden by the cover of dark night, was now appearing. Its rays were concentrating over the veil of darkness on the facility. They became lighter and spread around making way for sunshine to reach the darkened Earth.

'Hear me Sun, the king of all planets. I beg you for your light. Please, give us your light and save us', he said looking up at the first light of the morning.

A great burning filled all the sky after his words; fire glowed everywhere vaporising the walls of water and the steal of the building shone so bright that it blinded everyone. Nobody dared to look on the face of the light that emerged like never before from the rising sun faraway. In the moment of the morning, light answered for Jim's plea.

Rahu's shadow was getting burnt. 'No! It can't be', he cried as he saw his body vanishing. Rahu stumbled and just as he fell, he started to crawl for his life. His foul tongue had withered into ash. He was fading and dragging his body away from everyone.

The light burnt the tentacles and they were greatly becoming steam and joining the air of the sky. From great heights to the bottom of the river, every drop of wrathful water became one with the atmosphere and the furious wind that just emerged from the east blew it away. Finally, as the light dawned on Moon, her wrath also went away with it. She calmed down; her eyes turned to normal and she gained her senses.

Rahu, at last when his strength vanished, turned painfully towards Jim. The thing that went through his head other than the realisation of defeat was how the hell a human ever had the best of him.

'No! Foul human… I will not let this happen', he screamed.

Saturn seeing him crawl and suffer spoke, 'Why do you persist? Why keep fighting against us when we remain neutral to you? You believe your thirst will be quenched once you gain rulership of Earth; we all know it will never come to be. Why do you not accept that we will not allow you to cause destruction? You can see it now that it is pointless to keep fighting. You must know it by now that we planets have united and will continue to stay till *Asuras* like you try to bring harm to our world'.

Jim stepped up to him then. 'Why do you exploit the freedom that God has given you? Look what has your obsession gotten you to?' He looked at him and then an irksome laugh started to come from the fallen Rahu—half pained, half joyed. 'Your laugh won't justify your actions; they are both meaningless and purposeless. Your dream is as false as the shadow that you are—it will never have a form'.

He let a cackle of triumphant laughter on him. 'This is not over human. My purpose here is served. I will be back and I will have my…' Before he could whole his vengeful words, he disappeared and his cloak fell upon the Earth, bodiless. The eerie sense of satisfaction with which he had spoken put Jim in doubt.

The remaining dark shadow of the clouds had withdrawn after Rahu disappeared. Ketu was also nowhere to be seen. He sneaked past everyone's attention and escaped.

'Ja…Je…Jim…', Marshal spoke his name. His whisper caught Jim's ears and he hastened to him.

He went down on his knees. 'Marshal, don't worry Marshal, we'll take care of you', he was very anxious. 'Where's Moon? Somebody bring her. She can heal him right', he cried looking at the planets who were watching them helplessly. They didn't say anything. 'What's the matter with you? Somebody get her here fast'.

'Jim', Venus answered. 'He's… He's beyond healing now'.

Marshal's black eyes were fixed at Jim's tear-filled ones. Even though his body was in pain, the comfort of lying in his friend's arms gave him peace. He was counting his last breaths. The planets could only witness the grave loss. Marshal clasped his hand in Jim's hand and captured his eyes. Then he shook painfully, just a little. Jim knew but didn't want to accept it. There was utter quiet around them. Marshal waited for his final breath, looking at the drops of falling tears on him. He had saved the last of his energy to bid him goodbye. 'Don't cry, my friend. I fulfilled my promise. I was there with you, till the end of the line. Now it is time for me to say goodbye. You are the only one in my life who was like my own. Goodbye, my brother. Goodbye, my friend'. And then his eyes rolled up, and eyelids sank. The strength in the grip of his loosened. Jim still had his hand seized in both of his; he pressed his lips to it.

'Marshal… Marshal, wake up man. I need you. Come on Marshal…', Jim was speaking with choked throat. Then he looked at them and felt completely powerless. 'Is there nothing you can do? Please, help him'. They didn't say. He looked back at his pained face but there was a strange satisfaction there.

What is this sleep which holds you now? Why isn't it letting you go? You are lost in the dark and you cannot hear me. In my memory, I walk with you. There, I talk to you. The flash of your smile, your actions, your being there with me; I don't want to wake up from that dream because if I open my eyes, I won't find you there. I will know that you are gone and that will pain me. I don't want that pain.

'Jim, some people aren't meant to stay forever, no matter how close they are', Saturn had his hand on Jim's shoulder.

'Why does life have to take away the best from us? Why so early? Why can't we have someone stay a little longer?'

Mars came. 'His purpose of this life is over. Maybe somebody like you would need him after twenty years when he has grown up to be young, strong and honest, in another life'. Mars could feel his loss. Those tears rolling down the cheek had the saddest reality about them. He was empathising. *When life takes somebody away, the part of you that knows they won't come back again, starts to hurt you, real bad. The place and life you live in, is empty that they're gone and nobody can fill their place.*

Mars got up and turned towards back. Moon had finally approached them. She was gazing at Venus from afar. Mars looked at her now. She was standing at a distance, pondering. Then something clicked in his mind. He asked Saturn, 'She is thinking about it. Can she do it?'

Saturn's eyes became large in an instant. 'Of course she can, just like she did with us in her apartment', he also turned towards her. 'She's only considering whether she should or not'.

'I say she should', said Moon, advancing towards them.

'So do I', Mercury's voice also reached them. He emerged from behind them, pulling himself up. Saturn quickly helped him up. Mars reacted and took a fighting stance over his sight. 'It's ok', he looked towards Mars. 'No need to be cautious now. I am back to being me again'. Mars relaxed after looking at the other planets and seeing that they believed him. He came close to them with his hand pressing his ribs. He broke a few during the escape from Ketu's clutch.

She came near them. 'You do know that I do not do it for humans. That age is gone when I revived a living being back from the dead'.

'Yes, so it has been. But you brought us back from the dead', said Saturn.

'You're planets'.

'No we're not anymore', was the instant reply.

'I believe that Jim and his friend have done more to us than we imagined', said Mars.

'We will need him', said Moon. 'We will need them'.

At this, Venus nodded and went down to Jim. 'Draw away from the body. I will perform what no planet ever thought would be performed in this Kaliyuga'.

'I do not understand', said Jim.

'I will give him a second life'.

Jim could not believe what he had just heard. Moon took his hand and whispered, 'She's going to bring him back to life'. Jim was still in a state of shock. He turned his head up, not finding it realistic. His eyes fell on the one he needed the most at the time. Moon looked directly to him and said, 'Your friend will be with you in just a while'.

Jim found himself to be both shocked and surprised that he could barely stand still or hold a thought in his head. He also found fear lingering in the possibility of a failed attempt of Marshal's revival. It was the anxiety and fear only a man who could have his best friend resurrected could feel. Venus was at the start of a magical attempt whose conclusion was uncertain. She bent to her knees and held Marshal's head in her palms like a mother carrying her newborn carefully. Jim hoped to see Marshal make it across the death gate. He hoped to see his friend alive and hug him tight and cry on his shoulder. He hoped.

Venus looked at Marshal's forehead and began moving her lips slowly. The chant which only she had the knowledge of hearing and understanding, started to move the wind around them. It gained speed suddenly and a white light covered Marshal's feet. With more hymns, it climbed up the body. Everybody gazed at the wonder. Venus continued her spell and the light eventually reached the forehead. Moon was with her, she was also chanting something that she knew would heal the body once the soul is brought back in it. The light went away. They stopped and Venus stood up.

'Is it done?' asked Jim. They moved aside. He quickly went down and brought his face close to Marshal. 'Marshal… Can you hear me? Marshal speak up!' There were no marks of wounds on his body and the bruises, blood were gone.

For a moment there was no response from the body but then, he opened his eyes slowly.

'Marshal', he said ecstatic. As soon as the eyes opened, Jim wrapped him tightly in a hug.

'You're back Marshal. I can't believe it'. There were smiles on everyone's face seeing him back.

'Easy there, Jim', he said. Jim released him and his tear filled eyes had an amazing spark in them now. 'I thought I was dying'.

'They brought you back', he said. Marshal looked at them and got up with Jim's help.

'Thank you Venus, thank you very much', said Jim.

'You should thank her too. The soul wouldn't stay inside his body for too long unless Moon had healed him entirely', she said. They looked at her. She shook her head and told through telepathy that there was no need for thanks.

The next moment turned into a serious discussion as Mars raised a critical issue.

'It is not possible for Sun to do that to Rahu. The nature of our existence allows only Rahu to afflict Sun. The reverse cannot happen', he said.

'Then how did Sun erase him?' asked Marshal.

'He wasn't alone', came Saturn saying. 'I believe where Sun is, Jupiter is with him. Jupiter's power is expansion. Though I am not sure whether Jupiter has discovered his stone or not, Sun's extent of power confirms he has his ruby. And it seems Jupiter significantly expanded Sun's reach and power'.

'Not just that alone', Mercury said.

'Are you okay?' asked Venus.

'I can take care of that', Moon stepped up. She looked at his ribs and within a few seconds all his wounds were gone. Mars and Saturn withdrew a little, knowing that their presence would cause her harm.

Mercury looked at Jim and began speaking. 'Saturn's right. Sun cannot do this. Only Jupiter has the power to bring Rahu and Ketu under check. I do not know where, but they are together, at least for now. You can clearly see that Sun back there surpassed his human limitation. It is because he got the first Ruby. You must have learnt', he looked at Jim and Marshal 'we have powers in human form but they are much limited. I was able to find that once we came on Earth as humans, our precious individual first gemstones too came and spread throughout the planet. If we are able to find each of our gemstones, we can become far more powerful; the impact of our presence and aspect will be controllable. Somehow, Sun has managed to find his Ruby with the help of Jupiter and that is how he was able to help us like the way we saw'.

'Why did Rahu say that his purpose was served? What did he mean by that?' asked Jim.

'I am afraid we all have been played. All of this, catastrophe on the Earth through my intelligence has been a distraction. Both Rahu and Ketu were sent here by someone and they achieved their task'.

'Who sent them? What do they intend to do?' asked Moon.

'I don't know yet but it is something beyond our imagination', he said.

Jim thought that he might have an answer; he started walking away from them.

'What's with him?' asked Mars.

'Oh! He's just imagining... He's a writer, right? Let's see what he comes up with', answered Marshal.

As Jim moved significantly away from them, his mind gave him the last meeting with God. He looked straight into the now risen Sun and saw someone approaching him.

Chapter 18

For Jim, it was an extremely pleasant sight to see God come to him again.

'Hello Jim. It is so good to see you', he said. Jim was about to utter but God interrupted. 'What I am about to tell you now is most important. It will stay with us and the planets cannot know till you meet the tunnel maker. You want to know something. You may ask now'.

'Rahu's last words, were they false or true?' asked Jim.

'Only a few ill deeds have been done and more will be given life. If the *Devtas'*, he was looking at Jim who looked back at the planets after the mention, 'that is the planets are here, then the *Asuras* will also come'. He stood there, aghast. His feet felt to him as shaken. 'You have been caught in a net of deceit. Rahu and Ketu could not destroy all of them together and they knew it. They were only testing the extent of their powers so they could prepare an army of *Asuras* once they are unleashed from the flamed space of the parallel world'.

'How is that possible? Rahu and Ketu are never obedient to anyone. Who in the world has managed to control their obedience?'

'Again I will say, it is up to you to find that. Look behind you once more; for so long the planets have believed that it is only their great power that can hold the enemy in check. But I have found something in you. It is the small everyday deed that really curbs it. Faith in me, that keeps the darkness at bay. Act of love and sacrifice, one like that was made by your friend Marshal for you. I have never really told you why I chose you. To be honest, I didn't. They did. Because they knew that you give them something they lose at times: hope'.

Jim's realisation was a great surprise to him. 'They chose me?' he asked. God smiled. 'Sometimes seeing all this happen, I wish that it was someone else who had been chosen'.

'So would anyone else but it is not on you to decide that. The most important thing to decide is what to do with your time, imagination, courage, to know the good of all and that you are doing the right thing. And it is an encouraging endeavour'.

'What must we do now?'

'Find the stones of power. They will advance their powers and let them control their aspects and influence through presence. If it weren't for Sun and Jupiter, your doom was certain a while ago. You saw how greatly the stones have given powers to them. You also saw that even with a stone of power, Moon was angered and in her wrath she lost her sense of direction. The most important step you must take is you must be together. Unite with the two. Find them. For now, rejoice as you have stopped a certain calamity and all of you have a direction'.

Jim's mind was wrestling with him. And then wonder took him and a great joy he felt. All the eyes of the planets followed his gaze. Even though it was sunrise, the reflection of the moon was twinkling by the river. The falling water of the river over the demolished tunnel was murmuring loudly on the stones of the foot of the hill.

'They are thankful to you', God's voice whispered only in his ears. He had disappeared now. 'Only your will could have held them this long. This quest was never a test for you Jim. It was a learning lesson for them'.

Jim could hear their thoughts all of a sudden. The first thought that reached his mind was that of Mars's. 'We asked God why he loves humans dearly. Now we have our answer', he was talking to the other planets. They were together and listening to the talkative Mercury who went on to explain his ordeal.

Then it was Venus's. 'We may be planets that govern your existence; we take you from life to death and then to life again and then to salvation. But we also need you. The creation of God is big and we need each other in it'.

'I realised what a great change you can bring to us in an instant. I hope for a change and I know a good one will come with you around us'. This time it was Moon's thought.

'So, we just saved the world and nobody knows about it! That's just great'. Surprisingly, now came Marshal's thought. Jim turned to Saturn but he wasn't thinking anything. The expression on his face was of contentment. 'Thank you', was all Jim could hear.

He lifted his head up and his gaze reached the beautiful sky of the morning. God's face emerged there. He was watching them. He had a smile on him. And then it vanished. It gave him a moment of satisfaction. He turned around and began walking with the others. It was time for them to head back home, using the same spell they came there with.

Chapter 19

Jim was back at home. Kathryn was the happiest to see him and Marshal. Leia was sleeping upstairs. He went there with them, opened the door not much wide so that light didn't fell on Leia. He looked around; there she was in a corner, in her small bed. He was about to take his first step inside when the whisper from the same unknown entity spoke.

It is time.

But Jim felt that it wasn't a whisper. It came from the inside. There was no one there. He frowned slightly, as though he was still trying to work out where else would the voice come from. He tried to close the door without a snap before him.

The lights of the room illuminated all by themselves and left the three in shock.

'Come here', a voice came from Leia. Silence fell as though her words had struck Jim dumb and shocked. He quickly dashed towards her. She was up but her eyes were not her own. They were completely black.

'Who… What are you? What have you done to my daughter?' he faltered.

Kathryn and Marshal looked at her. 'Jim… What's', before she could complete, the voice came from Leia. Her mouth wasn't open but her eyes were at them.

'I am the one who whispered to you, showed you the way. It was quintessential to meet you and be your guiding light from this point onwards as the one who has been with you has played his role'.

'Is that our daughter talking?' asked Kathryn, half frightened, half shocked.

'Who are you? Don't you dare harm my daughter', said Jim.

'I can see that your meeting with God has altered your personality and consciousness for the better yet you remain as naïve as any hopeless human. You have questions and I will answer them all. You will understand some and some of them you will not. I will start by answering the first that lingers in your mind'. Their eyes were wide open. Shocked, they were to the core but Jim and Kathryn were scared. They were afraid of a possible danger that could harm Leia.

'God's role in your life was about to get over and so he sent me for you. In order for you to unite the planets you needed a force that knows all. It is my whisper that has led you to a small victory in your quest, which now you may rejoice'.

'It was you?' he said.

'Undoubtedly and now that God will no longer come to you like he did, I had to take a shell to fulfill my purpose. The closest to you was that of your daughter. Her role in the survival of your world is far more important than yours. Therefore, I have rested my soul in her body. Do not be afraid; while I stay in it, I will protect it. Unfortunately for me, this body will take its time to grow and with the limitations inside, I come back from my dormant sleep only for limited time'.

'You haven't told me who are you?'

'Interesting. You are quicker than the others'.

'What others?'

'Your world has not been destroyed once but several times already. By whom; your intelligence should give you the answer'.

Jim fell dumbstruck. Words had left him completely. After a few moments, he finally spoke, 'How's it possible? How could the *Asuras* have destroyed the world so many times?'

'Life on this Earth is older than you know. It has a cycle and in that there are ages of mankind which we call Yugas. They start with Satya Yuga then Treta Yuga, Dwapara and the one that you live in is called Kali Yuga. You're the chosen one. You're supposedly the savior. I prefer counting from the emergence of the first savior to the next, which in this case is the seventh time'.

'What! Why didn't the planets tell us that?' asked Marshal. She looked at Jim who was in uninterrupted contemplation.

'There can only be two explanations. Either they deliberately didn't tell us or they don't know', answered Jim.

'Precisely'.

'That means each time the Earth and Parallel Earth are destroyed, the Planets and *Asuras* die too', said Marshal.

'Without life, they have no purpose and so they face erasure', she said.

'If what you're saying is true, is it happening all over again?' he asked.

'Yes indeed with the exception of the chosen one of course; that is you'.

'Tell me about this cycle and the ages'.

'After the age of the animals, the living beings start their journey in Satya Yuga and as civilisation grows, modernises, the age advances as well. What you must know is that in the current Yuga, there is much of ill and that is why the *Asuras* will eventually cross over. The cycle originally was meant not to end at Kali Yuga but restart with Satya Yuga with the deletion of *Asura* influence on your Earth but so far they have won this war'.

'How does it end? I mean how do they end life?'

'They don't'.

'Then who does?'

'Only one has the power to give birth, to preserve and destroy. God destroys Earth and the cycle is created again. And it won't stop till the age is preserved as it was originally meant to be'.

'Who are you? Tell me. How do you know all this? Why should we trust you?'

'I am the one who created the tunnel that connects your world to their world. Even though you are aware that someone is attempting to open it, only I know when and how it will be opened before all hell is released here. As far as trust goes, I see you're alive and you know it is because of me'.

'What tunnel? What's she talking about Jim?' asked Kathryn. Marshal had the same question on his lips.

'You haven't told them. You really are different; the only one who didn't tell others'.

'My dreams Kathryn; I told you that I see planets in them. I didn't tell you I see something else as well'.

'The *Asura* on the boat!' the tunnel maker said. 'Doom is inevitable Jim. But there's something different about you that pushes me to keep hope'.

'I would like to understand how life ends'.

'My tunnel is flawless, a work of art if you may call it, a masterpiece. It isn't possible for *Devtas* or *Asuras* to open it from one side. Nor both the sides, if they wanted they could only open it together. But they never do that. So the answer is different. This will come as a shock to you and I don't expect you to recover from it anytime soon. The only way it can be opened is for a pure soul to open it from this side'.

'Pure soul! No, it can't be right'. His body pushed back as if it got a jolt.

'Jim! What happened?' Kathryn grabbed him.

'As the ages of mankind passes, at the end of the Kali Yuga there is only one person left as honourable as the pure soul. And that is you Jim Morgan, the chosen one. Across all times this Earth has been created, only the chosen one has opened the tunnel and brought death to all'.

She continued, 'It is the consequence of an imperfection that is inherent in the chosen ones. There will come a time when your emotions and ignorance will take control of you Jim; that is destiny and you will choose to let the *Asuras* pass the tunnel. It is inevitable. You are here because Earth is about to be destroyed, its every living being killed and entire existence eradicated by God and on who's flawed choice—your own'.

'I am the one who destroys life?' he whispered, completely believing what she spoke.

'That's a lot of crap coming from your mouth', shouted Marshal.

'You can deny. I have already seen responses of denial six times and this one is no different. I do not want to waste time as I have only less than a minute left. Jim, if you want to stop it, you must kill yourself'.

'You shut your mouth now. I believe, you're an *Asura* trying to blind Jim with all your nonsense', Marshal was furious now.

'I kill everyone?' he whispered again, trembling.

'Jim won't listen to you, he's more sensible than you think him to be', said Kathryn looking at Leia with a saddened face.

'Shoot yourself now'.

'Kathryn, take her to the next room please', said Marshal.

'Shoot now'.

Jim saw Marshal's gun on him. His impulses quickly got him and he took the gun.

'No Jim', screamed Kathryn. He had pulled the trigger by now.

'Jim', screamed Marshal.

The bullet fell on the ground. An aura had coated Jim entirely—A black aura. He didn't die; the bullet didn't pass the aura.

'This is what I wanted to tell you. You can't die Jim. You are destined to bring doom upon Earth and you will do exactly that. There's no one who can stop you but this time I hope that you as the chosen one can stop yourself'.

'Shut up!' screamed Marshal

'It is time', she said. Her eyes became normal and they closed. Leia was back in her body but she was sleeping.

*****